Anything For A Suit

by Ann Michelle

ISBN: 9798804663873

Please visit my website:
www.annemichellesworld.blogspot.com

Introduction by Ann

—o—

Hi Everybody!

I originally serialized this in my newsletter, but I figured many of you would want to add it to your collections, so here it is. This story is a tad shorter than my normal stories, but I think you'll enjoy it as it's pure, irreverent fun! You don't need to read *Anything for an 'A'* to enjoy this one, in case you haven't, but it never hurts. Either way, William is in a whole new bunch of trouble this time.

This is what happens to poor William after his wild night trying to convince his professor, the lovely Professor Natalya Ivanova, to give him a passing grade. He got the grade, but sadly for William, his job offer fell through. Now he needs to fly to the other coast to interview for a different job. Fortunately, his roommate Sandy knows someone who can pick him up from the airport and let him stay with her until the interview. What could possibly go wrong? Well, as William is about to find out when he grabs the wrong suitcase... a lot.

I hope you enjoy William's crazy journey! As always, drop me a line to let me know what you think at: annmichelle@ymail.com.

With love,
Ann :)

Chapter One: "A Ride From The Airport"
—o—

William stepped off the plane.

"Welcome to the other coast," he said pensively beneath his breath.

He started up the jet way to the gate. The airport seemed nice, but he wasn't focused on that. He was thinking about the interview. After getting Professor Ivanova to give him an "A", he was guaranteed to graduate on time. With a job offer already in hand, he thought he was set. Then the company folded overnight and his future vanished. Fortunately, the Professor had an old friend who needed an engineer like William. The company was halfway across the country, but it was a good job. She got him the interview. The rest was up to him now.

"You can do this," he told himself.

He actually wasn't so sure.

William followed the crowd down the concourse toward the baggage claim. The concourse seemed to go on and on forever until they finally reached an escalator, which took them down several floors, judging by its length. At the bottom, William saw the luggage carousels to his left and a row of taxis out the door ahead. He wouldn't need a taxi, however. When his roommate Sandy found out he was flying out here for an interview, she called a friend who lived nearby and got her to agree to let him stay with her. She would be picking him up from the airport too. That made this all so much easier.

"It's always good to have friends," thought William.

A buzzer went off and the luggage carousel started. William watched hundreds of nearly identical pieces of luggage come rolling past. Like most of the others, his suitcase was dark blue. Unlike the others, however, he'd had the foresight to put a sticker on his so he could identify it. The sticker was a Mickey Mouse he had found in the campus bookstore.

"There it is," he said, seeing a dark blue bag with a Mickey Mouse sticker on it.

William grabbed the bag and started toward the door. A moment later, he was outside in the smell of jet fuel and car pollution. Airports always had that smell no matter how large or small they were.

He scanned the waiting cars, but didn't see her.

"Where is this girl?" he asked himself.

No sooner had he asked than a cute little hot-pink VW Bug pulled up in front of him at the curb. The car was *very* girly, with white seats, eyelashes over the headlights, and flower rims on the tires. On the back was a bumper sticker that read: "Drive like a girl!" The white convertible top was down.

"You William?" asked the young woman at the wheel.

"Are you Mandi?"

"With an 'i'," she said.

"That's the one."

"Get in."

William heard the trunk pop and he saw it open slightly. He went around the car and deposited his suitcase in the trunk. Then he hopped into the passenger seat and buckled his belt. The girl smiled and pressed the gas pedal to the floor. The Bug roared off.

"Thanks for picking me up," said William.

"Anything for a friend of Sandy," said Mandi.

William glanced at the young woman out of the corner of his eye. She was really pretty with long brunette hair, an aquiline nose, and soft brown eyes. Her skin was beautifully tanned. Like her friend Sandy, her style was rather Bohemian; she wore a maxi-dress with long vertical brown, white and red stripes, all outlined in black. On her feet were brown leather clogs with platform heels and brass rivets. Her nails were filed square and painted white. It was very stylish, but particular.

A chill ran down William's spine at the sight of the clogs. Sandy had made him wear an identical pair this morning – the continuing consequences of her having caught him in her clothes. The thought that he had worn similar shoes to those this pretty young woman wore made him feel funny and strange: they had something in common, even if she didn't know it.

"Thankfully, Sandy's not here to comment on them," thought William. He had no doubt she would have said something too. "She'd find it too funny to resist."

Mandi turned off the airport road and into normal town traffic. The streets were busy, but not as bad as William had expected, not that the traffic was on his mind at the moment. He was thinking about the interview. He worried he wasn't ready. What if they asked questions he couldn't answer? He needed this job... could he get it?

"So you're Sandy's roommate?" asked Mandi.

"Yeah."

She smiled curiously and glanced at William. "Do you like living with her?" There was something in her voice which caught William's attention. It was like she was fighting not to laugh.

"Yeah, sure."

Mandi nodded her head. She returned her attention to the road, but seemed to be struggling now not to smile. She was blushing slightly too. This was making William self-conscious.

"What?" asked William finally.

"Sandy said, uh... well."

"What?"

"That you wear her clothes." There came the giggle.

William's heart stopped. His face turned white as a sheet. "She told you that?!" he gasped.

"She may have mentioned something about it," said Mandi casually, as if the topic was unimportant. But at the same time, she smirked at him with her eyes. She thought this was hilarious.

"I never— but— I mean— it's not like that!" he protested incoherently.

"Not like what?"

"I don't '*wear*' her clothes!" he said sourly.

"She said you do."

"Well, not by choice."

Mandi giggled again. "But you *do* wear her clothes."

William squirmed in his seat. His face burned with shame. He'd been caught. "Yeah, I guess. I mean, she *makes* me sometimes."

"'Makes' you?" said Mandi with a doubtful laugh. "How does she 'make' you?"

"She tells me to do it."

"And you just do it? That doesn't sound like 'make' to me. That sounds like 'want' to me."

"I do not *want* to wear her clothes!" blurted out William defensively. "The problem is she could tell people about it and I can't have that either, so I don't have any choice. I have to do what she says so she won't tell people... *which apparently she's doing anyways*."

Mandi laughed good-naturedly. "It's all right. She tells me everything. We have no secrets."

"That doesn't make me any happier."

Mandi shrugged her shoulders indifferently.

"And if you really don't have any secrets," continued William, "then you know she's *making* me wear her clothes. It's not my idea. She just shows up with something like a dress or something and she tells me to put it on."

"And you do it like a good girl."

William felt like he'd been punched in the gut at being called a girl. He wasn't going to share that though. He also felt condescended to, so he pursed his lips (in part to hide his discomfort) and he sourly responded: "Something like that."

Mandi pushed the pedal to the floor once more with her clog to get through a yellow light. Well... maybe it was pink. When they were on the other side, she slowed again. "What happens after you're dressed?"

"What do you mean?"

"I mean, then what? What happens after she 'makes' you put on her clothes?"

William shrugged his shoulders. "Nothing, really."

"Wait a minute," said Mandi incredulously. "You're telling me she just comes to you and tells you 'put this on' and hands you a dress and some heels and whatever else and then you do it and she just walks off?" She shook her head. "No, that doesn't make any sense."

William sank as deeply in the seat as he could. "I don't want to talk about it."

"I do. This is really weird. I want to know more." Her voice was bubbly and excited, not insulting.

"Well, there isn't more to tell."

"Oh yes there is. What does she make you do?" asked Mandi in a little more demanding tone.

"Nothing," said William sharply. "Like I told you: *nothing*."

"And like I told you: I don't believe you."

Mandi jerked the wheel and turned the car down a side road. They quickly ended up in a residential neighborhood which contained a mix of old, single-family homes and small apartment buildings. The area was awash in trees and the street was crowded with parked cars. They were zipping along, which was starting to make William nervous. Mandi didn't seem bothered in the least.

"So spill, *girlfriend*."

"There's nothing to say," said William.

"That doesn't make any sense," countered Mandi as the little pink Bug dashed between parked cars, pot holes and oncoming vehicles. "She must make you do *something* if she's making you wear her clothes. Otherwise, what's the point? Unless you're lying and you wear them because you want to."

"She *makes* me wear them. It's not my idea!"

"Then what does she make you do?!" demanded Mandi.

"Nothing!"

"Does she make you dance for her or something?" She pulled one hand from the steering wheel and shook it near her crotch like she was throwing dice, indicating that the kind of "or something" she suggested involved a certain sexual act.

"Absolutely not!" insisted William in blushing embarrassment.

"That hit a nerve. That must be it."

"It's not!   I do not *jerk off* for her entertainment!" William said this with intense disgust and made the words "jerk off" drip with disdain. "All I do is bring her drinks and clean up and stuff like that. That's it."

Mandi let out a piercing laugh; she had tricked him into admitting the truth. "Ha! Got you!" she proclaimed. Then she smiled contemplatively. "So you're her maid, huh? That's awesome! I could use a sissy maid."

William was completely flustered. How had this young woman he didn't even know managed to delve so deeply into his darkest secret? She seemed very good at getting under his skin. But, of course, she had inside information from Sandy to help her. Fortunately, she didn't seem to know everything. She didn't know, for example, that William had cross-dressed in Sandy's clothes from time to time even before he was caught trying to sneak out to see Professor Ivanova that night. That was still secret.

"Listen," said William, determined to defend his masculinity. "I don't know what Sandy told you, but none of this is what you're thinking. She *makes* me wear her clothes. That's it. I don't do it because I want to. She makes me. I'm not a sissy. I'm not a cross-dresser."

"Then how did she catch you in the first place?"

"What do you mean?"

She cranked the wheel and the Bug did a ninety-degree turn at high speeds down another side street. "She *caught* you, right? That's your story: you were blackmailed. Well, being *caught* implies that you were already doing it when she stumbled upon you. That means you were wearing her clothes when she found you, which means she didn't *make* you. Ergo, you're a cross-dresser."

"I am not," insisted William even as he marveled at her logic.

"Then why were you wearing her clothes?"

"It wasn't my idea." That was true. His cross-dressing the night Sandy caught him had been at the Professor's orders, and William decided to admit that now to keep Mandi from digging deeper. "I had to convince a professor to change my grade. She said she would do it if I, well, if I did some things for her. Part of that involved dressing up like a woman and going to her house. *Since I'm not a cross-dresser*, I didn't have any girl's clothes. That's when I borrowed Sandy's clothes. That's also when she walked in and *caught* me."

"Uh huh," said Mandi doubtfully.

"And everything since then has been because Sandy blackmailed me."

"Uh huh."

Mandi slammed on the brakes slowing the car to a crawl instantly and tossing everything forward. Then she cranked the steering wheel to the right and jerked the car into a small parking lot behind an apartment building, where she took the spot next to the backdoor.

"That's a great story, but I'll still bet you're a cross-dresser," she said.

"I am not."

Mandi shrugged her shoulders, grabbed her purse – a heavy brown leather bag that struck William as the size of a duffle bag – and got out of the car. William watched her move around the car and heard her heavy wooden platform clogs striking the pavement: **THUNK! THUNK! THUNK! THUNK!** He got out of the car now as well and met her at the trunk. She had it open already and was staring down at his suitcase. She began to giggle.

"What now?" asked William defensively.

"Not a cross-dresser, huh?"

"No. Why?"

Mandi pointed to the suitcase. "Minnie Mouse?"

"That's a sticker I bought to make my suitcase stand out from the other bags, and for your information, it's *Mickey Mouse*," said William smugly.

"Is it? Then why is Mickey wearing a red dress with white polka dots and yellow high heels?"

William's eyes dove to the suitcase. Sure enough, there was a Minnie Mouse sticker on it, not a Mickey sticker and she was indeed wearing a red dress and yellow high heels. "That can't be!" he gasped. He attacked the latch on the suitcase and snapped it open. The suitcase popped open. Inside were women's clothes. Suits, dresses and high heels.

He had the wrong suitcase... and his suit was nowhere to be seen.

His interview was not starting well.

Chapter Two: "The Wrong Suitcase"
—o—

Mandi picked up a neutral-colored high-heeled pump out of the suitcase. It had an open toe and a half-inch platform. The heel of the shoe had to be about five inches high and it had a thick decorative leather strap with a buckle over the vamp. It was an elegant shoe, a professional shoe, but also a sexy shoe. It was also not the sort of thing any non-cross-dressing male would ever carry in a suitcase. *Ever.*

"Sexy," said Mandi with a chuckle. Her chuckle sent jolts of shameful discomfort shooting down William's spine and made him squirm all over again. "Still claim you're not a cross-dresser?"

"It's not mine!" protested William.

"It's in *your* suitcase."

"This isn't my suitcase!"

Mandi laughed accusingly; his claim seemed ridiculous. "I'm supposed to believe it's just a coincidence that you put a 'Mickey Mouse' sticker on your suitcase," she said, complete with air quotes, "but someone else on the flight has the identical suitcase and just happened to put a 'Minnie Mouse' sticker on theirs, only for you to grab it 'by mistake' because you couldn't tell the difference between Mickey, in his shorts, and Minnie in a girly dress? How many 'Mouse' stickers do you think are out there? Do you know the odds on that?"

"But that's what happened!" It actually was.

"And you couldn't tell the difference between Mickey and Minnie? Really?"

"I was distracted. The place was awash with people and suitcases. I saw a mouse and didn't look at which one it was," said William. "I swear this really isn't my suitcase!"

"I don't believe you," sang Mandi.

"But it's true!"

It didn't seem that way to Mandi though. "I think the truth is you're a cross-dresser, just like Sandy says, and you put the Minnie Mouse on your suitcase because it gave you a little thrill or whatever, and you decided to travel out here with a suitcase full of women's clothes—"

"Why would I do that?"

Mandi shrugged her shoulders. "You tell me."

"I wouldn't do that! I need to interview! Why would I do this?"

"Maybe you're interviewing as a woman? Maybe it just turns you on? How do I know? I've never met a cross-dresser with a Minnie Mouse fetish before? Do you dress like Minnie too?" she asked with an enormous grin. "*M — I — C.* See you in heels," she sang.

William was stunned. Was she just playing with him now? "Stop that."

She didn't. "*K — E — Y.* Why? Because it excites you!"

"Stop that," said William again, which only made Mandi's grin grow.

"*M — O — U — S — E.*" Mandi laughed and held up the high-heeled shoe in front of him and shook it playfully. "You're going to look sooooooo cute in this for your interview."

"*It's not mine!*"

"It's in *your* suitcase."

"That's not mine either," snapped William in an exasperated tone.

"Just admit it. You're a cross-dresser. Look, it's cool. You can wear all this stuff at my place all you want. I don't mind. It might even be fun. And if you want, you can be my sissy maid just like you're Sandy's sissy maid if that's what makes you happy—"

"*None of this is mine!*"

Mandi rolled her eyes and ignored him. She fingered the skirt from a wheat-colored skirt suit in the suitcase. "You do have pretty taste."

"It's not mine," pleaded William helplessly.

His tone struck her. Mandi considered this for a moment. It was *possible* he was telling the truth. It seemed unlikely, but it was possible. It was much more likely he was playing some game with her... but it was possible. Maybe it was just a coincidence that Sandy had caught him in her clothes. And maybe it was just a coincidence that he had run across a Minnie suitcase instead of a Mickey suitcase and he grabbed it. And maybe it was just a coincidence that it was full of women's clothes that seemed quite appropriate for a kick-ass interview. Maybe. Yeah right.

Still, she decided to give him a chance. "All right. Prove it."

"How?"

"We'll go upstairs and you can put on your girly clothes," said Mandi waving her hand over the suitcase. "If they're not yours, then they won't fit, right? But I'll bet they fit like a glove."

"Fine, I'll prove it," snapped William. He was sure they wouldn't fit. After all, what were the chances that the woman who owned this suitcase was the same size as him? It wasn't like he was a standard-sized woman.

"Let's go," said Mandi.

"Fine."

William grabbed the suitcase and pulled it from the trunk.

"If they fit," cautioned Mandi as William lifted the suitcase to the ground, "I expect you to be a good little sissy maid for me, just like you are for Sandy. I could use a maid to clean my place. And if that maid happens to be a boy in a dress... *a Minnie Mouse dress,* then all the better."

William glared at her. "Well, I hate to break this to you, sister, but these clothes will never fit."

"*Sister?*" repeated Mandi with an incredulous laugh at his use of outdated slang before mockingly countering with equally outdated slang: "Oh zap, girlfriend!"

William blushed. "They won't fit. You'll see," he grumbled.

"Yep. We will."

With that, he grabbed the suitcase and he and Mandi made their way upstairs to her apartment. He was determined to prove that these weren't his clothes. After all, they weren't.

Mandi hummed the Mickey Mouse theme song the entire way.

—o—

William heaved the suitcase onto the bed and opened it. Once again, he saw the wheat-colored skirt suit and the neutral open-toed pumps. It was a pretty suit, for a woman. He had no desire to wear it though. In fact, he had no desire to ever wear women's clothes ever again, especially after his recent experience. Yeah, he had some cross-dressing instincts, but after the past week and now this, he was finished with women's clothes. He was swearing that off!

"None of these are going to fit," he said.

"We'll see when you try 'em on," said Mandi who stood at the foot of the bed with her arms folded. She was sliding her foot in and out of her clog and periodically brushing her hair back over her ear as she watched. She couldn't help but be excited. She'd never seen a boy in a dress up close before. She wondered how she would feel about it. Hearing how Sandy made William cross-dress had actually been a bit of a turn-on for her, but she wasn't sure if she would feel the same way in person. She was about to find out though.

Meanwhile, William pulled out the skirt bottom for the suit. Then he grabbed the suit jacket and a white blouse. He set those aside. Beneath, he found a sundress in bright yellow, orange and blue. It seemed to be paired with some red strappy sandals. Beneath that were panties, some lingerie, some stockings and then some toiletries. He put all of it on the bed.

"Why are you unpacking the whole thing?"

"I want to see if there's something in here identifying the woman whose suitcase this is. If there's an ID or something, then I can show you that this isn't my suitcase," said William.

"But there's nothing."

"Sadly, no. The luggage tag got torn off too."

"Then there's only one thing left to do."

William sighed. He didn't want to do this, but he did want to prove these clothes weren't his. He didn't like people thinking he was a cross-dresser, even people he barely knew like Mandi. That was a shameful secret he wanted to remain a secret. Besides, if she thought these belonged to him, she would tell Sandy who would become even more unbearable.

"Quit stalling," said Mandi.

"All right," said William and he picked up the skirt.

Mandi licked her lips. She was enjoying this already, just the act of making him squirm as she had. It gave her a thrill. She couldn't wait to see her first live boy in a dress (or skirt). Her nipples were hard and her lower regions warm.

William looked at Mandi in silence for several

seconds as if he was waiting for something. "Aren't you going to leave?" he finally asked.

"Leave?"

"Yes, so I can try these on."

Mandi scoffed. "Are you kidding? If I leave then you claim that none of it fit. Forget it. If this stuff fits or not, I'm going to be right here to find out, Princess," she said. The truth was, she was too excited to leave. She wanted to see all of this from start to finish.

William furrowed his brow. "What about my privacy?"

"Doesn't apply in this situation. Now change."

"You're going to have to leave," insisted William.

"Oh, no. This is my apartment. My rules."

William licked his lips. His loss of privacy would have been a minor problem, truthfully, except that the idea that this pretty young woman, so very giggly as she was, would watch him strip down and try to slip into a woman's skirt made him very horny. That made his penis grow hard. Unfortunately, that complicated things. It was bad enough she would see him try to slip into the skirt, but seeing him slip into the skirt with an enormous erection wagging around all over the place as he tried was an order of magnitude worse. That would be *really* embarrassing. Moreover, he particularly didn't want her to watch as Mandi seemed eager to explore this and he didn't want to give her any ideas.

"Will you please leave? This is embarrassing enough as it is," he said.

"I'll bet it is. But I'm not leaving. Get on with it."

"I can't, not with you watching."

"You get dressed in front of Sandy all the time. You can do it in front of me too."

"That's different."

"How is that different?"

William blushed. The answer was that Sandy

blackmailed him, which gave her the power to demand it. Mandi had no such power over him. "She makes me do it," he said softly, not wanting to spell it out further.

"Well, look at it this way," said Mandi. "I'm making you do it now too."

"How's that?"

"Duh! *Blackmail!* If Sandy can blackmail you, then I can blackmail you too," said Mandi with an enormous grin.

"No, you can't," said William.

"Why not?"

"There's nothing you can blackmail me with."

"Said the boy with the Minnie Mouse fetish. Think about it, Minnie. There's lots I could use!" said Mandi eagerly.

William imagined several ways she could blackmail him, from his needing to stay at her place until he flew home to his needing to get a ride from her to the interview. Plus, who knows what she knew from Sandy? He decided not to push his luck on this. Besides, something inside him did very much want to prove that these weren't his clothes and that he did *not* have a Minnie Mouse fetish. He decided to proceed; he would just need to be careful not to expose his erection to her.

"Fine," he said, trying to feign indifference.

"Good boy."

William shuddered at her perky yet condescending tone. There was something horrifically cute about this young woman that just disarmed him. It was almost enough to make him want to run away while he could. But he didn't. Instead, he grabbed his belt and unbuckled it. A moment later, his jeans fell to the floor. He simultaneously kicked off his fashionable sneakers and then stepped out of his pants. This left him in his white briefs; he turned slightly to show

Mandi his rear so she couldn't see his erection tenting out the briefs. He then grabbed the short skirt and unzipped it. He held it out before himself.

"Hold on," said Mandi.

"What now?"

"Take off the underwear, Minnie. You'd never wear those under a skirt and I'm not having you sabotage this test."

William burned with embarrassment, but he did as he was told, keeping his rear to Mandi so she couldn't see his now-throbbing erection. He stepped out of his briefs, leaving them on the floor.

Mandi whistled and laughed. "Nice butt."

William's shame became a few degrees hotter.

Mandi then leaned over to one side. "I see balls," she sang, as she looked between his legs.

William's shame shot off the charts. He tried to ignore it and held out the skirt again. It was time to do this and get it over with. Prove his case and move on. He glanced down at the skirt and felt dizzy for a moment: he couldn't believe he was going to put on women's clothes *again*. First the Professor. Then Sandy. Now Mandi. Why did this always seem to happen to him? What was wrong with these women? Each of them?

Either way, he stepped into the skirt and pulled it up his legs, hoping it got stopped at his knees or thighs and this silly idea ended before it began. It didn't though. He managed to pull it past his knees. Arg. Then it slipped over his thighs. Double arg. Finally, it came all the way up to his hips... and then over.

"Crap," thought William.

It seemed to fit.

"*Interesting*," said Mandi.

William shook his head. "No, it's, um, too loose."

Mandi stepped over behind him and zipped it up. The skirt now fit perfectly. It was snug. It hugged his curves. It hung to just above his knees and it looked very good on him. In fact, it looked like it had been tailor made for him. William's heart sank when he saw this in the mirror.

"That's just a coincidence," stammered William.

"Uh huh," said Mandi doubtfully.

"It is!" he protested. "I'll bet the rest doesn't fit!"

William frantically stripped off his shirt and grabbed the blouse. He was sure that wouldn't fit. After all, women and men just aren't shaped the same. Women had breasts. He didn't. Women had hourglass figures. He didn't. There was no way this blouse would fit.

Mandi watched him with an ever-growing smile.

"So this is a boy in a dress?" she thought. She tingled deep inside.

William hurriedly pulled the blouse over his shoulders and started to button it up. It was a tad bit loose around the chest where the owner's breasts would be, but otherwise it too fit like a glove.

"Strike two," sang Mandi.

William felt his stomach drop. This was not going well. He had one shot left at this point: the shoes. His feet were bigger than most women's feet. Heck, the time he bought his own shoes when he was younger, he had to buy them from a specialty store! Hopefully, the owner of these clothes had tiny feet. He grabbed the pumps and tossed them to the floor. Then he maneuvered his right foot into one of the pumps and pushed it inside. To his horror, the shoe fit perfectly.

All the color left his face.

"Looks like the shoe fits, Cinderella," said Mandi with a chuckle. "And that would be strike three."

"It really is a coincidence," said William in a

defeated tone.

"Is this a coincidence too?" asked Mandi and she grabbed for his crotch. Before William even knew what was happening, she had latched her hand onto his erection which tented out the skirt. She squeezed it hard through the skirt, causing precum to dribble out into the skirt. She then let go.

"That— my— you touched—" he sputtered.

An embarrassed William desperately tried to cover his erection with his hands. It was far too late for that though. All he could do now was stare at her dumbfounded that these clothes had fit and that she had grabbed his erection. More precum dribbled into his skirt.

"You grabbed my dick," he said in disbelief.

"Yep."

"You just grabbed it!"

Mandi smiled and held out her hand toward his crotch. "Want me to do it again?"

William actually heard something inside himself scream, "YES!" but he knew that wasn't a good answer. He needed to stop whatever this was from spinning out of control. He had to get a handle on all of this – no pun intended – before he ended up being used by Mandi like he was being used by Sandy. He needed to get back to focusing on his interview and cutting out all other distractions. He could not afford another distraction today!

"No."

Mandi chuckled. "All right. Well, word of advice: don't point that thing at someone unless you intend for them to use it."

"I'll try to remember that," said William sourly. "Now, if you don't mind, I'd like to change back into my *own* clothes and go rest up. I need to start thinking about my interview."

Mandi shrugged her shoulders. "Ok. Do you know what I find funny though?"

"What?"

"You claim this isn't your suitcase, but you've never asked me to take you back to the airport to see if they have your 'real' suitcase. Doesn't that seem a little strange to you?"

William licked his lips nervously. He hadn't thought of that. In all the excitement, it hadn't occurred to him to do that. He felt like he'd been caught in a lie now, even though he hadn't lied at all, and he could have disproved it so easily! He felt foolish. There was no way she would believe he wasn't a cross-dresser now. Even worse though, her comment brought back into focus a huge problem he had: he needed to go get his suitcase. Without that, he had no suit for the interview.

"Can you take me back to the airport?" he asked sheepishly.

Mandi snickered. "Yes. Yes, I can... my little cross-dresser."

William shuddered.

"But there's one condition," she added unexpectedly.

"What's that?"

"You need to go in the clothes you're wearing right now."

Chapter Three: "Back To The Airport"
—o—

"There is *NO WAY* I'm wearing these clothes to the airport," said William.

He was shocked Mandi had even suggested it. Not only were these women's clothes – and the idea that he would walk into an airport wearing them ludicrous – but these were the clothes of some unknown woman whose suitcase he had taken by accident. Wearing women's clothes would be bad enough. Wearing *these* clothes seemed even crazier! It seemed perverted somehow... kinky. Oddly, it seemed kind of exciting too, but he put that thought out of his head.

"Then I'm not taking you," said Mandi flatly.

"What?!" gasped William. "You can't do that! I need my suitcase!"

"It's my car. It's my time. I can put any conditions I want on it. If you don't like it, then call a cab or something."

"I don't have the money," protested William.

Mandi rolled her eyes. "*Students!*" she scoffed. Then she shook her head determinedly. "Doesn't matter. If you want a ride from me, then you're going to wear that suit."

"Why?"

"Because I want to see that. I think you look cute and I think it would be fun." "Cute" was probably the wrong word on her part; it was a little misleading. What she really meant was that the more she saw William in the skirt suit and heels, the more turned on she became and the more she wanted to explore this whole cross-dressing thing. She was starting to understand what Sandy saw in keeping William feminized around her apartment.

William saw things a little differently. He saw disaster from trying to pass himself off as a woman at the airport, perhaps even of an epic scale: fingers point, screams arise, a mob forms, torches are lit, there's a chase, there's an arrest, incarceration, a cellmate named "Big Cock", and of course, no job. He shook his head vigorously. "I can't go out in public dressed like this!"

"Why not?"

"Why not?!" gasped William incredulously.

"Yeah, why not." Her question was genuine.

"Because I can't!"

"That's not an answer. Besides, you do it for Sandy."

"That's different."

"How?" asked Mandi with a hint of annoyance. As she saw it, if he could do it for Sandy, he could do it for her.

"It just is."

"You did it for that professor too."

"That's different too," grumbled William.

"No, it's not. You wanted something from her, now you want something from me. So you go in the skirt or we don't go." She folded her arms to signal that she would not budge on this point.

William saw the determination in her eyes. "Crap," he thought.

He took a deep breath to calm himself and tried once more to convince her.

"I need that suitcase," he said tensely.

"I know," said Mandi.

"If I can't get my suitcase back, then I can't get my suit. If I can't get my suit, then I can't interview. See the problem?"

"Sure do."

"If you don't take me, then I can't get my

suitcase."

"Yup."

"That's why you need to take me," said William.

Mandi shrugged her shoulders. "That sounds like a 'you' problem, not a 'me' problem," she said. She rubbed the sensual, soft blouse material between her fingers. "As I see it, you have two options. Either you wear these clothes and we go to the airport together and collect your suitcase... or you wave your suit goodbye and you wear these clothes to your interview. What's it going to be, buttercup?"

A chill raced down William's spine. He needed this job. It was his future. He couldn't play around with the interview or let anything mess it up for him, and showing up in women's clothes would definitely mess it up. He could never do that! That meant he had no choice now but to pay Mandi's humiliating price and wear the stupid skirt suit to the airport. He took a deep, frustrated breath. Seriously, why did every woman in his life suddenly want to put him in dresses? He didn't get it.

"All right," he said reluctantly.

Mandi smiled, lighting up her whole face. That was easier than she expected. Maybe Sandy really was onto something about him liking it, she thought! "Great," she said. She picked up her purse and started toward the door. William didn't follow though. "Why aren't you coming?"

"I almost hate to say this... but if I'm going like this, then I need makeup. A wig. Some underwear. That sort of thing."

Mandi scratched her chin thoughtfully. She walked back over to William and opened her purse. From it, she pulled out her lipstick and painted his lips. Then she pulled out some eye shadow and mascara and gave him a quick touch-up. A moment later, his face looked reasonable feminine. Indeed, she marveled how feminine he looked for a boy and how easily that had happened.

"There," she said.

"What about a wig?"

"I don't have one. You'll just have to be one of those women with short hair." She ran her fingers through his hair and made it spiky. It wasn't much, but it was an approximation of a Pixie cut at least. Fortunately, the rest of him was feminine enough that few would doubt he really was a woman. She added some hairspray to hold it in place. Then she saw a pretty broach in the suitcase. She took it and pinned it to the suit coat. "There. Perfect."

William wanted to protest, but he didn't see the point. He wasn't going to win; he held none of the cards and she was already headed toward the car in any event. "Let me look through the suitcase for some underwear and then we can go," he called out.

"You don't need underwear," she called back.

William furrowed his brow again. "Say what?"

Mandi stopped and turned back. "You don't need panties."

"Yes, I do."

"Who are you planning to show them too?"

"No one," said William incredulously.

"Then you don't need them."

William blushed. "It's not the panties that I'm worried about," said William with some embarrassment. He pointed toward his crotch and blushed even deeper. "It's *it* that I'm worried about."

"*It*? What about *it*?"

"What if *it* gets hard? Without some underwear to hold *it* in place, *it* could poke out the skirt or even pop out beneath it!"

"By '*it*', I take it you mean your—"

"*Yes*, that."

"Then don't get hard," said Mandi simply.

William looked stupefied. "It doesn't work that way."

"It doesn't?"

"No."

Mandi rolled her eyes. "Okay," she said and she hiked up her maxi-dress high enough to get her hands underneath. She grabbed her own tiny yellow panties and worked them down her body until she could kick them off. "Now neither of us has panties. Feel better?"

William glared at her. "No."

"Oh well, that's all you're getting," laughed Mandi and she grabbed a brown leather purse, tossed William's wallet into it along with some makeup, and handed it to him. "Let's get going."

—o—

The Bug raced past several blocks of restaurants and small, quaint shops as they shot through town. The road had two lanes going in each direction. Mandi's long hair was flowing in the wind; her foot was heavy on the gas. William tried to make himself very small as they zipped along so that people wouldn't see him. It wasn't working. It was hard to disappear in a hot-pink convertible Bug, especially with the top down. Everyone looked up as they passed.

"Don't you think you're going a little fast?" said William.

"Not really."

"You've got to be going double the speed limit!"

Mandi smiled wickedly and smoothly pressed her high-heeled mule harder against the accelerator noticeably increasing the speed of the car. "I thought you wanted to get there fast? I didn't know you wanted to dillydally on the road. Should we stop and do some shopping too?"

"Just pay attention. I'd like to get there in one piece."

Mandi laughed. "Does my driving scare you that much?"

"Let's just say I've worn heels enough now that I worry about someone in shoes like those controlling a car at speeds like these."

"Amateur."

"I think I know what you can and cannot do in heels!"

"And yet, you keep trying to tell me you're not a cross-dresser! Any other tips about women's clothes you want to share?"

William held his tongue. Nothing he could say would help.

Meanwhile, Mandi glanced in her rearview mirror. She saw a dirty brown Jeep with two young college guys catching up to the Bug on William's side. They slowed as they pulled level.

"We have fans," she said unhappily, nodding toward the Jeep.

William glanced over his right shoulder. He saw the two young men looking at him excitedly. They made no secret of their interest in these two apparently beautiful women. This worried William, who did not want to attract the attention of anyone, much less young men! Even worse, as their Jeep was slightly taller than the Bug, they could look down into the Bug and see most everything. They particularly seemed to be enjoying the view of William's feminine legs. This made William's penis grow for some reason.

"Hey angels," called the driver.

"Wanna get some drinks?" asked the other.

Mandi rolled her eyes. "What a horrible line!"

she yelled to William, but loudly enough that the two males could hear it. This didn't seem to bother them though. To the contrary, they smirked at each other and then broke into laughter.

William looked for somewhere to hide, but there was nowhere.

"Let's get away from them," said Mandi.

She sped up. Unfortunately, they sped up to stay with her.

"If you don't like drinks, I've got some *meat* you might like better," said the driver and he visibly slipped his hand between his legs and grabbed his crotch and thrust it toward her as best he could while driving.

"Gross. Guys like that drive me nuts," said Mandi to William.

"What do they want?" asked William.

"You're a guy, what do you think they want?"

William swallowed hard. That's what he was afraid of. "Can we lose them?"

Mandi shrugged her shoulders. "Probably. We'll just turn off at the nex—" A wicked smile appeared on her lips. She glanced at William and gave him the once over with her right eye. "Not before we teach them a lesson."

"Wh— what kind of lesson? What are you going to do?"

"Go with my lead."

"But what are you going to do?" asked William again.

"We're going to flirt with them."

"*Flirt?!*" repeated William incredulously. The last thing in the world he wanted was to flirt with two jerks in a Jeep. Heck, he didn't want to flirt with anyone, not dressed like this. He shook his head. "I'm not flirting. There is no way I'm flirting. I am *NOT* flirting with two guys in a Jeep. No way. Never."

"Yes, you are."

"I'm not."

"You're going to flirt because I want you to and this is my car and you want me to drive you to the airport. Embarrassing guys like that is a moral imperative. Now stop whining and follow my lead or I'll stop the car right now and let you try to talk your way out of things with them in person. Got it? Maybe they'll be nice enough to give you a ride to the airport."

That image made William shudder and tremble; it almost made him wet himself. He shook his head anxiously. "You can't do that!"

"Then do as I say!"

"I don't know how to flirt with guys!"

"It's simple. Follow my lead."

William kept shaking his head, but Mandi moved on as if she had gotten his consent. Apparently, he was committed whether he wanted to be or not under threat of being surrendered to them as bootie. "Well, how bad can it be?" he told himself unpersuasively.

"You boys like to party, do you?" called Mandi across to the Jeep.

"Baby, we are the party kings. How about we go back to our place?" responded the passenger.

Mandi glanced skeptically at both, pretended to look them up and down, snorted loudly, and then shook her head. "You two don't know the first thing about parties," yelled Mandi dismissively.

"*Oh contrier*," said the driver. "We know all there is to know about partying!"

"Do you? Ever done this?" asked Mandi and she leaned over and gave the surprised William a huge, sexy, wet kiss right on the lips, smearing their lipsticks all over his lips. His toes curled in his shoes and his penis shot to attention beneath his skirt. As he wore no panties, his penis jammed against his skirt and formed a small, but noticeable bump. Fortunately, the young men didn't notice.

"Don't— what— what are you doing?!" gasped William in shock as she pulled her lips away. He blushed terribly.

"Whoa!!!" exclaimed the two boys at the same time.

"Go along with me," whispered Mandi to William.

William wanted to tell her to forget it, but he imagined her stopping and kicking him out of the car for the boys to pick up. It was best to let her do whatever she was planning to do than face that. Besides, the kiss had shaken him and left him disoriented. He wanted to hate it, but it had been amazing, truly amazing! His whole body tingled and went limp all over, except in one area.

The boys in the Jeep watched in intense anticipation.

"Do it again!" yelled the driver.

Mandi ignore his request. Instead, she yelled, "Ever done this?" She then slipped her hand between William's thighs and ran her hand up beneath his skirt. William sucked in a ton of air and went tense. His erection jumped to full strength in her hand which kept it from being seen. It was throbbing.

"Whoaaaa!!!" exclaimed the two young men again.

"Start rubbing your nipples through your shirt," said Mandi so that only William could hear.

"What?!"

"Do it!"

William took a deep breath to summon his courage and did as she commanded. He moved his hands up to his chest and started playing with his nipples through his blouse. The two men stared at him with jaws open. They couldn't tell he had no breasts whatsoever.

"I don't see either of you boys touching anything important yourselves," called out Mandi. "Afraid to share?"

The two guys exchanged excited glances and then dropped their hands down to the waistbands of their shorts. Each had an erection, which each was holding within seconds. The driver was even stroking his.

"Much better, boys," said Mandi.

She started rubbing her hand up and down William's inner-thigh, ducking her hand beneath his skirt and then teasingly pulling it away. This was highly erotic and it was clear that both males were totally turned on by it, as was William. In fact, he was so turned on he had now become terrified that he might come if she pushed her hand too far up his skirt.

"You might want to stop!" exclaimed William anxiously.

"Just keep going with it."

"But—"

"Trust me."

William watched nervously as her hand dipped beneath his skirt toward his throbbing erection once more. She was *soooo* close. Things were about to get messy, both literally and figuratively. He would never live it down if he came; she would never let him. Even worse, he didn't understand what this was achieving. How was making him a masturbation fantasy for two college jerks going to teach them a lesson? To the contrary, it seemed to be giving them what they wanted.

William glanced over and saw both males playing with themselves now in the exposed Jeep. He felt deeply embarrassed. "Oh God, they're jerking themselves off over me!" he declared.

Mandi snickered. "Happens to women all the time."

"I'm not a woman."

Mandi looked her feminized visitor up and down out of the corner of her eye. He looked *very* feminine. He looked comfortable feminine too; not at all awkward in the skirt or heels. "Are you sure?" she asked. Then, before he could answer, she glanced forward and said, "Don't worry, we're almost there."

"Almost where?"

"Look ahead."

William looked ahead and saw that, coming up, the road split in two directions. The boys were so busy looking at them they hadn't noticed this yet. That meant each car would soon go their separate ways and that would be the end of this, mercifully. William still didn't see how this was any sort of revenge for womankind, however, if that's what Mandi was after.

"You like that, boys?" called out Mandi.

"Oh yeah, baby," said one.

"That's awesome," laughed the other.

"And you're both totally turned on?" she asked.

"You know it!"

"Well, there's one more thing you should know," said Mandi.

"And what's that, hottie?"

"Beside the fact it's 'au contraire' you idiot, remember this," she exclaimed smugly and she pushed William's skirt up exposing his erection. His stiff manhood popped into view. There it was standing tall in the breeze. Unmistakable.

Jaws dropped.

The cheering stopped.

The catcalls stopped.

The stroking stopped.

The young men stared at William's erection in

utter horror. William, who was horrified when Mandi first tugged up his skirt, now felt a warm sensation when he saw their reactions; it felt like justice to him. Genuine justice.   Mandi, meanwhile, grabbed his throbbing erection and wiggled it at the two young men.

"Hi there! I'm Mr. Pee-pee. Do I excite you?" she called over with a laugh, just as the road split.

William burst out laughing.

The shaken driver slammed on his brakes and the Jeep came to a smoking stop, to the consternation of several other drivers. William unbuckled his seatbelt and spun in the seat to watch the two young men. Neither one seemed to be moving. The driver sat there clutching the steering wheel in shock. Suddenly, they both exploded in heated argument. William imagined this would continue and what had happened would haunt their dreams, at least their fantasies, for some time to come.

"That... was hilarious!" exclaimed William.

"Couldn't happen to bigger jerks!" said Mandi. "Of course, the hard part was the timing." She glanced at his still exposed erection before adding, "One of the hard parts at least. Might I recommend sitting down again?"

"What? Why?"

Mandi pointed to his rod which was flapping around in the open air for other drivers to see. William blushed and yanked the skirt down over it, spinning around and sinking back into his seat.

"Punch it," he said.

"Your wish is my command," said Mandi and she pushed her clog into the gas pedal once more. It was off to the airport.

Chapter Four: "His Lost Luggage"
—o—

William and Mandi were second in line. They were at the lost luggage counter at the airport. William was nervous. He had been in public several times now dressed as a woman, but had yet to get used to it. He didn't think he ever would. It was just too nerve-wracking. Of course, he wasn't really hoping to get used to it either. To the contrary, he hoped he would never be in public ever again in another item of feminine clothing for the rest of his life, but frankly the odds of that seemed strangely low. Adding to his nervousness was the fact he wasn't wearing any panties. Wearing a skirt and no panties made him feel naked, even if it was a longer skirt. But of course, the skirt's length would do nothing to hide an erection if his dick decided to make an appearance, which he knew it would.

"I wish you'd let me grab some panties," whispered William.

"Big fan of panties, are you?"

"You know what I mean. What if I get hard?"

"I'm sure it will be fine... just give me plenty of warning so I can reach a safe distance."

"Ha ha," said William sourly.

"I thought it was funny too," said Mandi. He was so easy to tease, she thought with a smile. She glanced around the room again. There were lines of luggage against one wall, two counters at the front, and a glass wall running the length of the room beyond which cars passed on their way to pick up travelers. She glanced at William again next. She knew he was anxious, but it didn't show. It also didn't show that he didn't have much experience as a girl. He walked well in heels, carried himself with excellent feminine comportment, and displayed just enough confidence to be seen as comfortable as who he was, even if he wasn't the person he appeared to be at all... and wasn't the least bit comfortable. Honestly, he made an excellent girl and she found herself rather interested in seeing how he looked in lingerie. She had a sexy red teddie in particular that she wanted to see him wear.

"You really carry yourself well as a girl for being a boy," said Mandi.

William instantly tensed up; she'd said that a little loudly. In fact, she said it in her regular voice. William's head shot around to see if anyone had heard her. They hadn't. Nevertheless, he hissed, *"Don't say something like that!* Someone could hear you!"

"What if they do?"

"Then they would know!"

"So?"

William glared at her. "What do you mean, 'so'?"

"I mean 'so.' What do you think they're going to do? Call the police? Scream and pass out? They're not going to strip you naked and shove a red hot poker up your a—"

"Can we please not talk about this?!"

Mandi snickered. "Ok. But you do walk really well for being a boy. You're great in heels."

"Thanks," grumbled William. "Sandy makes me practice."

"Really?"

"Yeah. She doesn't want me 'stomping around' anymore, she says."

"Well, she trained you well."

William ignored her compliment. The woman in front of them had just been called to the counter. He stepped forward and looked around, trying to see if anyone had spotted him. Fortunately, the room was largely empty and no one seemed to pay him much attention; though when they first arrived at the airport he thought he had gotten some strange glances walking from the parking garage. He still didn't know if those people saw through his disguise or if they thought he was attractive, neither of which alternatives made him happy actually.

"How often does she make you practice?" asked Mandi.

"What?" asked William.

"Practice. How often?"

"An hour a day, but that was before," said William. He kept glancing around. "Can we please not talk about this?"

"You seem nervous," observed Mandi.

"Because you won't stop talking about this!"

"It's no big deal. Nobody cares."

"They'll care if you tell them I'm a man!" snapped William now also a little too loudly. His eyes shot around anxiously once more. Fortunately, there was no one nearby to overhear his slip-up.

"Who's telling everybody now?" said Mandi in a told-you-so tone.

William glared at her. *"You are."*

"Want me to lift your skirt again?" laughed Mandi.

All the color drained from William's face. Would she really do that? Here? She'd done it before. "Don't you dare."

"You liked it, admit it."

"I did not!"

"You were hard as a rock when I did it," countered Mandi. She pointed at his crotch: "Those things don't lie about that; you were *X...cited.*"

"Next," called the man in the blue uniform behind the counter. William was relieved to stop Mandi from continuing this conversation. He was also relieved that he would soon have his suitcase and be out of here.

He needed to get away from being in public and, even more so, he needed to get somewhere he could focus on preparing for his interview; the Professor had warned him they might ask him technical questions and he needed time to review his class notes.

William stepped up to the counter.

The man didn't smile. He barely even looked up from his computer. "Luggage tag."

"I don't have it."

The man looked up and sighed. "You don't have the luggage tag?"

"No. Sorry."

"Do you have your ticket and some form of identification at least?"

William nodded. Then he pulled open the large brown purse Mandi had made him carry and fished out his ticket. He handed it to the man and then returned to his purse to find his wallet. In the meantime, the man noted the flight number and then checked his computer. They did indeed have three suitcases from that flight that had not been claimed.

"Tough flight," said the man.

"What do you mean?"

"We don't normally have so many bags go wrong from one flight. They must have had a computer glitch or something. Do you have your ID?"

William found his wallet. From it, he pulled his driver's license. He handed it to the man. He hadn't really thought about the fact he didn't exactly match his driver's license at the moment when he handed it to the man.

"*This is you?*" asked the man incredulously.

William bit his lip, realizing his mistake. "Ug," he thought. He hoped the man would handle this professionally and quietly.

No such luck.

"Hey Ted," said the man to the man at the counter next to him. "Check this one out."

"Now wait a minute," objected William.

"Just relax, *Ma'am*," said the man snidely. "We have this handled." He then stepped over to his friend and showed him William's identification. The other man put his hand to his mouth and tried to suppress a laugh.

"*Damn!*" said the other man.

William felt himself shrink. This was humiliating. This was what he feared about coming to the airport in a dress – well, that and a mob with pitchforks. But what could he do now? He stood there helplessly.

"Is there a problem?" asked Mandi, who stepped between the counters and now confronted the two men face to face.

The first man looked Mandi up and down. "This says your friend is a man."

"He is."

"He doesn't look like a man," said the first man.

"Neither do you," shot back Mandi as coldly as an icy mountain lake.

William put his hand on her shoulder. "It's all right, I'll handle it."

Mandi pushed his hand away and focused on the employee. "Why don't you do your job and get on your computer and find my friend's missing luggage before I decide to report you to your manager?"

"Report away," dared the man.

Mandi raised an eyebrow. "You're saying that won't help?"

"Nah, go ahead and call him," chuckled the man.

"I see," said Mandi. Then, with one lightening fast move, both of her hands shot out from her sides and grabbed each of the two men by the crotch. She squeezed her hands shut and her grip became a vice. Both men doubled over. The first one nearly fell to his knees. "Do I have you attention now, boys?"

"Yes," gasped the first. "Yes! Absolutely!"

The second one nodded his head in agreement.

"Good. Because I don't like people making fun of my friends. So now we're going to move back over to your computer and you're going to run a search for my friend's suitcase, got it? And if there's another disparaging word, I'm going to rip something off each of you. Understood?"

"Yes— yes, Ma'am," said the first.

The other man nodded. He looked ready to burst.

Mandi inched the group several paces to the left where the first man could work the computer. The entire time, she held on to both of their manhoods, through their pants, with an iron grip. They were clearly in agony. Mandi, however, was smiling mischievously.

"These are the second and third ones of these I've held today. I'm starting to get used to this," said Mandi pleasantly. There was no hint of stress or anger in her voice. She seemed quite calm. If anything, she sounded pleased or amused.

"I'm glad," said the shocked William.

"It's funny that boys come with these... kind of a controller, really. And they say women are the weaker sex. Ha! There's probably an on-off button somewhere inside your butts too."

William snickered at the absurdity of this. He'd never seen a woman grabbing a man by his penis in his life, much less two at once. And the ridiculous smile on her face and the nerd-like commentary... it all made William laugh.

"She leads a charmed life," he told himself.

He looked around to see what the people around them were doing. By pure chance, the small room had temporarily emptied.   There were a couple women watching from a luggage carousel way down the hallway, but he doubted they could see what Mandi was doing exactly. That seemed to be about it in terms of people paying them any attention.

"A charmed life indeed," he told himself.

"Your bag isn't one of the ones we have," announced the first man through painfully clenched teeth after entering William's information in his computer.

William stepped forward to the counter. "You don't have it?!"

"No. Someone must have taken it."

William furrowed his brow. "What kind of jerk takes someone else's luggage?"

"Yeah, what kind?" asked Mandi rolling her eyes.

"What do you mean?"

Mandi nodded at the skirt suit he wore.

"Oh, yeah," said William in an embarrassed tone as he recalled wrongly taking the Minnie Mouse suitcase.

"I can give you a form to make a claim, but if you wait a couple days, people almost always bring them back once they realize their mistake. If you want to leave a phone number where we can reach you, we'll contact you once it comes in," said the first man. His voice sounded hoarse.

"We don't have time for that," said William.

"Why not?" asked Mandi, still maintaining her grip on both men.

"You don't understand. My suit was in there! I need that for the interview tomorrow morning. I can't wait."

"Oh right. Buy a new suit."

"I don't have money for a new suit!" William's whole future employment life seemed to be flashing before his eyes owing to a lack of pants. He had no idea what to do now.

Mandi frowned. "I don't know what to tell you." Then she perked up. "Wear the suit you've got! It looks good on you."

William glared at her. "Are you kidding?"

"You'd be memorable."

"Not in a good way."

"Who knows, maybe this is exactly what they're looking for? An outside the box thinker!"

"Can you please let us go now?" pleaded the first man.

Mandi blushed. "Oh yeah. Sorry. I forgot."

She let go and the second man immediately fell to his knees. He proclaimed "Damn!" and then crawled behind the counter quite possibly to die. The first man grabbed his crotch also and started rubbing it, through his pants of course, to soothe the pain.

Mandi turned back to William. "So what do we do?"

"Can you loan me money?"

Mandi shook her head. "I barely have gas money."

"What am I going to do?"

"I don't know."

Unnoticed by either Mandi or William, a tall blonde woman with exquisite taste in clothes walked up behind them. She wore an emerald green calf-length A-line dress with silver platform designer sandals with a thick heel and a double t-strap. On her fingers were several expensive rings. Diamond earrings hung from her ears.

"That's a lovely suit," she said.

William turned to face her. "Uh, thank you."

"You know, of course, *it's mine.*"
This day just kept getting better all the time.

Chapter Five: "You Have My Suitcase"
—o—

William stared in shock at the gorgeous woman in the sharp emerald green dress and the tall silver sandals; gorgeous in a Cruella de Vil sort of way. She radiated confidence. She radiated danger too. William found himself rather intimidated; this was not someone you crossed. Mandi too looked nervous. She and William exchanged worried glances.

"What's yours?" asked William nervously. His mouth had gone dry.

"That suit you're wearing is mine," said the woman.

William swallowed hard and looked down at the wheat-colored suit he wore with the tight knee-length skirt and the tall neutral open-toed pumps. This was a disaster... *another* disaster. How in the world could he be so unlucky, he wondered? How could the owner of that suitcase be here right now at this very instant? And how was he going to get out of this? He decided it was best to deny everything and hope for the best.

"These are *my* clothes," insisted William.

Mandi nodded her head helplessly.

The woman snickered condescendingly. "Hardly."

"Wh— what makes you say that?"

"For starters, *young man*, you aren't even a woman. You're a boy. And those clothes were not made for you. They were made for me. They were made specially for me."

William's jaw dropped. How did she know he was a boy? No one else knew! Well, no one knew until they read his drivers license or until Mandi flashed his erection at them... but apart from that, no one knew! Practically no one.

"How— how did you know?" he asked cautiously.

"Very few women have six-inch bulges in their skirts. Or is it four inches?"

Mandi raised a curious eyebrow and leaned over to one side to look around William at his crotch. She saw the bump and smirked. "I'm thinking four is more like it," she said.

William blushed. "I've never measured."

"I'm sure," said the woman coldly. "Where is my suitcase?"

"Hold on! How do we know these clothes belong to you?" demanded Mandi. "You're a lot taller than William and thinner, but they fit him. That means they won't fit you!"

"My dear, if they didn't belong to me, I wouldn't be asking for them, would I?" said the woman rhetorically.

"Touché," said Mandi.

"Can you describe them?" asked William, still looking for an escape.

The woman rolled her eyes. Then she looked William up and down. "Wheat-colored skirt suit with a white blouse and open-toed designer pumps handmade in Italy. Is that what you mean? Oh, and the purse isn't mine. I'm assuming that's second hand or something. K-mart."

Mandi blushed in embarrassment. "Hey! That's mine."

The woman smiled coldly, which made Mandi shrink away.

"Well, anyone could have described the clothes like that," said William, taking up where Mandi had surrendered.

"How else would you like me to describe them?" said the woman with growing annoyance.

"I don't know. Tell me something not everyone

in this room could see just by looking at them."

"Very well. There's a label on the inside—"

"There's no name written inside these."

"I didn't say I'd written my name in them like some child's underwear when they're away at camp. I said there was a label. The label is from the tailor who made these items *for me*. What's more, the broach you are so proudly wearing is a family heirloom."

Both William and Mandi glanced at the broach.

"Now, I've proven to you that these are mine and I am in no mood to continue this argument. So are you going to give me my suitcase or do I need to call over those two police officers and have you both arrested for trying to steal it? Let me caution you that the broach alone will constitute grand theft."

William and Mandi looked to where the woman pointed and saw two police officers moseying about. They looked bored. They looked like they would enjoy the excitement of arresting a cross-dressing thief and his panty-less accomplice. It seemed best to avoid involving them.

"Look," said William. "This wasn't my choice."

Mandi rolled her eyes. "He says that a lot."

"It really wasn't. My suitcase got taken by mistake. I took yours by mistake. I thought it had a Mickey Mouse sticker on it, but it was a Minnie Mouse. I didn't realize that—"

"You couldn't tell the difference between Mickey and Minnie?" asked the woman incredulously.

"That's what I said," said Mandi.

"I was in a hurry," said William defensively.

The woman shook her head. "All right," she said. "That explains why you took my suitcase. Now explain to me what part of that explanation led you to decide to open my suitcase and try on my clothes? Surely, you wore your own clothes on the plane. Or you could have worn your friend's clothes if you felt the need to be a woman." She pointed at Mandi when she said this.

William cast his eyes to the ground. "It was kind of a dare."

The woman stared at him. "So you're an idiot to boot."

"Yeah," said Mandi. "He is."

"And I suppose it was *your* dare," said the woman rather accusingly to Mandi.

Mandi blushed and bit her lip.

"I'm really sorry," said William.

"So am I," added Mandi.

The woman rolled her eyes again. "Heartwarming," she said sarcastically. "Just give me back my suitcase so I can be on my way. You two can go steal suitcases to play dress up to your hearts' content after that."

William and Mandi glanced nervously at each other once again.

The woman's brow darkened. "What?"

"We don't have it here," said William.

"It's at my apartment," said Mandi.

The woman exhaled frustratedly. She took several seconds to process this before she spoke again. "All right," she said firmly, leaving no doubt this was a command, not a proposal. "Here's how we're going to handle this. You're both going to give me your identifications, car keys, wallets, whatever else you are holding. That way, you can't run away. Then we're going to your apartment to collect my suitcase."

"And if we refuse?" asked Mandi cautiously.

The woman smiled a bitter smile. Both William and Mandi got the message.

William nodded his head. "All right."

A moment later, they handed over their identifications and wallets and walked outside with the woman. When they stepped to the curb, a black car appeared. It wasn't quite a limousine, but it was very nice and roomy. It had a driver too. The woman climbed into the back and they followed. The woman handed Mandi's driver's license to the driver and he took off toward her apartment.

As they drove, the woman kept eyeing them. William and Mandi both felt uncomfortable. They felt like children caught with their fingers in the cookie jar who now awaited some punishment. There was nothing they could do, however. They had been separated from their car, their keys and their money... what little they had of it. The woman had their names and addresses too. If she called the police, they could be in serious trouble. All they could do right now was obey.

"I take it you're a cross-dresser?" said the woman as they made their way through town.

William blushed. "Why does everybody think that?"

"Duh," said Mandi. "Have you looked in the mirror lately?"

"Just because I'm wearing women's clothes doesn't make me a cross-dresser."

"No, but you must be a cross-dresser," said the woman.

"I'm not. This was just a dare, like I said."

The woman shook her head. "The way you walk in heels suggests practice... lots of practice. Moreover, there's stubble on your legs, suggesting you shaved them. But it's several days old, which suggests you shaved your legs a few days ago. Hence, you didn't just shave your legs to put on my clothes. There are traces of nail polish on your cuticles too. That means you painted your nails recently, but took it off, again before you put on my clothes. Clearly, you've dressed as a woman before, recently in fact, and before you stole my suitcase."

"You go, Sherlock!" laughed Mandi.

William turned bright red with embarrassment. "I'm not a cross-dresser," he said futilely. "I've just had a couple of unfortunate things happen to me recently. None of it was my idea."

"This was your idea then?" asked the woman of Mandi.

Mandi shook her head. "No. I only met him today. But don't let him fool you, he's a cross-dresser all right."

"*I am not!*"

"Either way, you look phenomenal," said the woman.

"I do?!" William hadn't expected a compliment. To the contrary, he'd expected her to mock him or act disgusted or something along those lines. The last thing he expected was the woman to say something nice to the young man who stole and wore her clothes.

"Yes. Most men look awful in dresses. They look uncomfortable and unshapely. They act overtly masculine to hide their embarrassment and overtly feminine in the belief they are acting like women. There is nothing natural about them. You, by comparison, act quite naturally. That makes you genuinely passable. If it weren't for that telltale bulge in your skirt, I would have thought you were a girl."

"I told you that you looked good," said Mandi.

William twisted his lip. This wasn't really something he wanted to hear. The idea that he was passable was an affront to his manhood, even if it had helped him maintain some dignity during the bizarrely large number of instances where he had found himself cross-dressed in public lately. And right now, his manhood was struggling, so this compliment was not well timed. Moreover, he certainly didn't want either Mandi or this woman getting any ideas about him being able to go out in public like this. The sooner he got back to the apartment and out of these clothes the better! He never wanted to see the inside of another dress in his life... if that made sense.

"I still look like a man," he said contrarily.

"No, you don't," said the woman.

"Not really," added Mandi. "Those guys in the Jeep didn't know."

"Jeep?" asked the woman.

Mandi snickered and explained. As she did, William sunk deeper and deeper into his seat. He looked out the window to avoid their eyes. By coincidence, they were just passing the spot where Mandi had flashed the two college guys with his erection. Part of him fought the urge to chuckle as he recalled their expressions, but the rest of him would rather forget that two men had masturbated over him, especially as Mandi was telling the story.

"Show me your erection," said the woman suddenly.

William jerked back to reality and glared at the woman. "What?"

"I want to see your dick."

"Why?"

"I need to see how photogenic it is."

William's jaw dropped. "You what?"

"I need to know how it will look on film."

"Why would my dick ever end up on film?" William shook his head vigorously. "There is no way I'm ever putting my dick on film, and there is no way I'm showing it to you or anybody else."

"I don't think we understand each other," said the woman calmly, but coldly.

"You got that right," snarled William.

"Why do you want to see his dick?" asked Mandi, whose curiosity had been piqued by the strangeness of the request. This wasn't just voyeurism. This was something more.

"I'm a photographer. The clothes you stole are not 'my clothes' in the simple sense that you think. They were meant for a model. I had those clothes made for me by an expert tailor to fit my model perfectly," said the woman. "He was coming in with them in his suitcase, but he wasn't at the airport when I arrived and he's not answering his phone now. I suspect he left when he couldn't find the suitcase." Neither William nor Mandi had yet picked up on her use of the masculine pronoun to describe the model. They assumed she meant the tailor was bringing them in.

"How does that affect me?" asked William.

"The clothes fit you like a dream, we can all see that. And obviously, you're very pretty as a woman. So I've decided I want you for my photo shoot. You're going to be my new model."

William and Mandi's jaws both dropped. Was this woman truly suggesting that he pose for photos in women's clothes? Did she really want him to act as a model for whatever she was doing? That was ridiculous, thought William! He was a man! There was no way he could – or would – model women's clothes!

"Me?! No! No way," said William. "No one is taking pictures of me in women's clothes."

"I am," said the woman.

Mandi chuckled at the thought of poor William posing for photos in women's clothes and couldn't resist adding her sarcastic two cents: "Make sure you send me copies of the photos. You're going to look so cute in all those dresses and skirts," she laughed.

"You're not out of this either, my dear," said the woman.

Mandi twisted her lip. "What do you mean?"

"I need *two* models for this particular shoot and you're perfect for what I need as well."

"Me?!" exclaimed Mandi. "Forget it! I look horrible in photos. The camera adds like forty pounds to my frame and gives me zits. Trust me, you don't want me in any photo you're going to take."

"You'll be fine."

"Yeah, you'll look cute," said William snidely, parroting back Mandi's comment to him.

Mandi smacked William on the arm with the back of her hand. "Look at what you got us into with that stupid suitcase."

"Me?! You made me wear the clothes!" shot back William.

"You didn't have to agree!"

"You weren't going to let me out of it!"

"*Children*, behave," said the woman calmly.

They stopped arguing. William then sat up straighter. "Listen lady," he said, "you don't want me. I'm a guy. I have a dick. It can pop up at the most inopportune times." He glanced at his crotch hoping for a timely display of this, but his penis wasn't cooperating. "Either way, you don't want me. I'm a guy. You want someone who looks natural in women's clothes – *a woman*, for example!"

"No, you're what I'm looking for."

William bit his tongue. Was this woman crazy? What kind of photo shoot would use a man wearing women's clothes? No matter how much she thought he was passable, the truth would be obvious on film. You just can't hide a thing like that, he told himself. He hadn't yet connected the fact she wanted to know how his penis would look in photographs.

"This isn't going to work," said William.

"You let me decide that."

William exhaled unhappily again. "All right, let me be even more clear. I can't do this. I have an interview that I need to get to tomorrow. I don't even have a suit anymore since my suitcase is gone, and I don't have any money. I need today to figure out what I'm going to do about that. I can't waste any time today doing some crazy photo shoot."

The woman snickered.

"What?" asked William.

"Then this is truly your lucky day. I happen to have a large collection of excellent suits at my estate. When you're done with the photo shoot, I'll let you have one. You will also be paid for your time," said the woman. She then looked at Mandi. "As will you."

Mandi and William glanced at each other. Mandi saw the chance to get gas money and maybe a little more. Maybe she could even buy this shawl she'd had her eyes on for the past few weeks. As for William, despite his recent aversion to all things feminine – on him at least – this sounded like the only realistic solution he had to the suit crisis. That made this something he needed to consider. He *needed* a suit for his interview and this got it for him; no other options seemed available. Getting paid on top of that would help too. He still wasn't sure though.

"What are the photos for?" asked William.

"What do you mean?" asked the woman.

"Are they going to be in some fashion magazine or something? Who's going to see them?"

"Do you care?"

"No," said Mandi, even as Williams said, "Yes" at the same time.

The woman smirked. "They're going into my private collection. No one will see them."

"No one?"

"Correct," said the woman.

William raised an eyebrow. This woman was going to pay them to take photos just for her private collection? She was nuts. Who would do that? On the other hand, this did mean he never had to worry about anyone he knew stumbling across the images and recognizing him if they were locked up in the vault of some crazy woman, not that he was likely to be recognized anyways, not in a dress and makeup.

"I guess that makes this easier," he told himself.

"What do you think?" asked Mandi.

William shrugged his shoulders, but his eyes said "I think so." He really had no choice.

"I'm behind on my rent," said Mandi.

"And I do need a suit," admitted William. "I have no idea where else I'm going to get one today... and with no money."

"Everyone wins," said the woman.

Mandi shrugged her shoulders. "What could be the harm?"

What indeed?

A few minutes later, the car pulled into the parking lot at Mandi's apartment building. The driver pulled into a spot and went inside to find the suitcase. The woman let Mandi go with him. William wanted to go inside and change, seeing as how his male clothes were there, but the woman refused. Mandi and the driver came back with the suitcase almost immediately. They had only stopped to repack the suitcase. After this, the driver backed out of the lot and made his way out of town, up into the hills where a number of very wealthy people had large estates. William and Mandi were curious where they were headed, to say the least.

Chapter Six: "Her Collection"
—o—

It took forty minutes to get out of town and reach the estate, which was located in the middle of a series of rolling hills with a view of the ocean in the distance. There were other estates in the area, but none were close enough to matter. The estate itself consisted of a main house, a pool house and two guest houses. The main house was enormous. It struck William that it might be almost as large as the on-campus apartment building where he lived. It was gorgeous too. The outside was done in a style evocative of an Italian villa. The inside was filled with expensive classical furniture. The woman had great taste.

The woman left them in the front hallway as she went to check on something.

"Wouldn't you love to live here?" said William to Mandi. He was awed by the premises. Mandi wasn't.

She shrugged her shoulders. "A lot to clean."

"That's why you need a maid."

Mandi chuckled. "Are you volunteering?"

William didn't understand. "Me? Why me?"

"I figured you'd like the uniform."

"Ha, ha," said William sourly.

"Have you noticed the paintings?" asked Mandi. She pointed to the painting right across from them in the entranceway and to several more down the hallway. The house appeared to be filled with them.

"What about them?"

"Take a closer look."

William walked around examining the paintings. They were all surreal, suggestive, and interesting. There was something also vaguely sexual about them. The one hanging in the main hallway, for example, almost looked like a giant, squarish, pierced nipple.

Almost. A few feet down the hall, there was one that could have been a deconstructed male chastity device. *Could have been.* It looked like a metal grill or perhaps a cage, shaped a little like a banana. The one across from it was, well a little different.

"What does that look like to you?" asked William through twisted lips.

Mandi snickered. "I think it looks painful."

"Does that really look like a high-heeled shoe to you?"

"Uh huh."

"And a—"

"Yep."

"And she's stepping on it!" shuddered William with some degree of horror.

"You've never had yours stepped on? I hear it's all the rage," said Mandi with a laugh and she stomped the heel of her platform clog against the Italian tile floor of the hallway. *THUD!!*

William cringed. "I can't say that I have."

"When we get home, you can slap yours on the coffee table and I'll step on it for you."

William winced. "I think I'll pass."

"You have no sense of adventure," scoffed Mandi.

William examined the nipple picture. Up close, it was actually harder to see it for what it was than from a distance. It kind of looked like a pinkish moonscape with a silvery arch across it. But even a few steps away, it became obvious what was being suggested.

"Why do you think she has these paintings?" asked William.

"I don't know. Interesting mystery though, isn't it?"

"Spooky."

William seemed to be getting increasingly

nervous as he examined these images. They were suggestive of something he couldn't quite put his finger on and that bothered him. What did they tell him about this woman who had so strangely insisted on photographing him, a male, in women's clothes? He didn't know and that worried him. After all, he was the one who would be in the dresses in the photos they were about to take.

Unlike William, Mandi didn't seem nervous, but she was certainly curious. To her, this was all a puzzle worthy of solving, but nothing to worry about. But then, she wouldn't be the one wearing the dresses in the photo. Well, she would be wearing a dress, but that was different.

"What do you think this means?" asked William.

Mandi shrugged her shoulders.

Before either could speak again, however, the woman rejoined them. She then walked them through the main house. Each of the paintings they passed along the way had similar themes to those in the front hallway.

"What's the deal with the paintings?" asked William.

"I'm a collector," said the woman.

"Of what?" asked Mandi.

"Of whatever I find interesting."

The woman opened a set of French doors to a large marble patio. The patio was roughly the size of Mandi's parking lot and it hosted a crystal clear rectangular pool, a heart-shaped hot tub, and a shaded cabana. It was ringed with perfectly-spaced fruit trees through which you could still see the surrounding countryside. William had never seen anything like it. It was like some ancient Greek temple on a hill top overlooking distant villages.

"This is gorgeous," said William.

"We'll be shooting some of the photos here," said the woman. "The rest we'll shoot upstairs in the main bedroom."

William and Mandi looked around. This didn't seem so bad. The location was gorgeous. Everything looked high class. The air was fresh. It seemed the perfect place for a photo shoot. This gave both a good deal of confidence, especially with the promise of payment and William's desperately needed new suit tipping the scales of judgment. It still bothered him that he would be modeling women's clothes for some reason that didn't make much sense to him, but he also realized that no one was going to see the photos, so it didn't matter if Cruella was a little strange.

"Are you ready to go inside and begin?" asked the woman.

William and Mandi exchanged glances. They nodded their heads.

—o—

The woman led William and Mandi to the master bedroom. William didn't normally notice these things – well, he never used to at least – but she walked amazingly well in her high heels. She moved confidently without any wobble. He did not, despite all the recent experience he had garnered. He almost wanted to ask her how she did it, but with any luck, this would be the last time he would ever wear heels in public, and he really didn't want to know.

"This is kind of exciting," said Mandi. "I've never done a photo shoot before."

"Me neither," said William nervously.

"I think you'll enjoy it," said the woman. She smirked at William. She still couldn't believe he walked so femininely or that he wore the dress so femininely.

She was impressed.

"Do you do a lot of photo shoots here?" asked Mandi.

"Some."

"Are they all sexual?"

The woman smiled knowingly that Mandi had figured that much out. "Some."

"And you're sure no one will *ever* see these?" asked William for the fifth or sixth or seventh time.

"Yes, William. Your secret is absolutely safe."

William nodded his head, but didn't feel any less nervous. Letting his photo be taken in women's clothes went against all his greatest fears, even if he wouldn't be recognizable. What if someone saw the photos and figured out who he was? Of course, the chances of that were tiny – zero basically – but the possibility still troubled him and that made this difficult.

They started up a wide staircase with red Persian-carpeted runners. William took the staircase with remarkable ease despite his tall heels. They had proven surprisingly comfortable for being such tall heels. At the top of the stairs, they walked down a hallway until they reached the master bedroom. The room was larger than either of their apartments. It was decorated much like the rest of the house with an enormous bed in the middle of the room and suggestive paintings on the walls. French doors opened to a balcony. Standing before the bed was a short man with a ponytail and two cameras hanging from his neck.

Mandi nudged William with her elbow. "A photographer. Do you think he works for a real magazine?"

"Yeah, Humiliated Morons Monthly."

"Oh, you get that too?"

William shot Mandi an evil look. She winked back.

"Don't be so serious. This is fun," she said.
Mandi was clearly enjoying herself; she had all day.
William was not; he was a nervous wreck. Lost luggage,
a skirt suit, no panties, busted, busted, busted, and now
this. This had been a rough day for him and it wasn't
over yet. Indeed, the closer they came to starting the
photo shoot, the more scared he got. He just kept
telling himself that he needed the suit and that no one
would see these photos.

"Here are our models," said Cruella to the man
with the ponytail.

"Lovely," said the man, looking Mandi up and
down.

Mandi smiled. "Hi."

He then looked William up and down. "Perfect."

"Why don't you take the young lady to the other
room and get her changed? I'll get William ready," said
the woman.

William cringed at being outed as a man, but the
man with the ponytail didn't respond to this revelation
at all. Instead, he merely nodded and took Mandi to
another room. Meanwhile, the woman in the emerald
dress marched William to a closet bigger than his
bedroom and showed him a rack of clothing, both
women's and men's. William again marveled at how
attractive she was, and how intimidating.

"Perhaps you'd like to pick out a suit," she said.

"Any one?"

"Any one. Men's or women's, it's up to you."

William looked around. There were a huge
number of suits here and most were of very high
quality. He ran his hands over the selection and slowly
pulled out three or four that he liked. *Men's*, of course.
He finally settled on a three-button checkered black suit
that he knew would look amazing. It was young,
fashionable, and yet respectable, perfect for an

interview.

"I'll take this one," he said.

"Excellent choice. Now let's go earn it, shall we?"

With that, the woman took the suit and carried it out into the bedroom, where she hung it over the back of a chair. It would remain visible there as an incentive. Then she motioned for William to move toward the bed in front of the camera.

"What are you wearing beneath the skirt?" asked the woman.

William blushed. "Not much."

"Lift your skirt and show me."

"But I'm not even wearing panties!"

"Show me."

"I'd rather not."

"*Lift your skirt and show me.*"

William bit his lip. This all seemed too much. But then, this was what it would take to get what he needed. And frankly, if he was being honest with himself, this wasn't nearly as weird or as difficult as the things he had done for his Professor to get his grade improved. So, if this got him that precious suit, then he would do it. He took a deep breath and slowly pulled his skirt up as commanded. His erection popped out the bottom of the skirt, as he did. It was now visible in all its glory... however many inches that glory really was.

"That will do nicely," purred the woman.

Click.

Chapter Seven: *"En Garde"*
—o—

As was said, William pulled his skirt up and exposed his manhood for the woman with the camera to see. The attractive woman, in a domineering sort of way. The woman whose dress William liked, not that he was in to that sort of thing, and whose stolen shoes he thought were surprisingly comfortable for heels. And she apparently liked what she saw too.

"That will do nicely," purred the woman.

Click.

"Nicely for what?" asked William.

Click click.

Before the woman could answer, if she intended to answer at all, Mandi burst through the door wearing a black "Lone Ranger" mask which covered an inch or two around her eyes. There was a wicked grin on her face. It wasn't her face, however, that drew William's attention. Mandi still wore her black, red, brown and white-striped max-skirt and her brown high-heeled platform clogs, but to this, she had added a black strap-on belt with an enormous plastic penis jutting out from it. The penis was a fluorescent pink which likely glowed in the dark. It was at least eight inches long. William was shocked to see it.

"Say 'ello to my little friend!" exclaimed Mandi.

William's jaw dropped. "Mandi?"

"None other," laughed Mandi. She was clearly delighted.

"Where did you get that?!" gasped William.

"Oliver gave it to me," she said and she pointed to the photographer. She then swung her hips around like she was playing with a hula-hoop, causing the plastic penis to swing back and forth, thrusting on several directions. It was all vaguely hypnotic.

William shot a worried glance at the woman. "You're kidding?"

"Afraid not."

"You never said anything about— *that*!"

"Did you think I just wanted a photo of you standing around in a dress? I could have taken that at the airport."

William bit his tongue. He was trying to decide if the suit was worth it given this new information. He knew it was. He needed that suit. His entire future depended on it! Plus, no one would ever see what happened next – somehow he seemed less sure of that suddenly, but he clung to it in his internal argument. Still, this was a shock, and Mandi's uh, *enthusiasm*, was not making it any easier.

"I guess—" he started to say.

He stopped mid-sentence, however, as Mandi started making noises like a bumble bee. She was even flapping her arms at her sides as she slowly danced toward him in a zigzag pattern. "Zzzzzzz!"

"What are you doing?" asked William firmly.

"Can't you guess?" She was getting really close. "Zzzzzzz!"

"Seriously, what are you doing?"

"Zzzzzzz!"

"Stop that!"

"Zzzzzzz!"

Mandi was now only three or four feet away. She then danced right up him and poked him with the plastic penis. "Doink!" she giggled. Then she stepped back and spread her hips and shoulders wide, causing the plastic penis to jut out straight before her. "*En garde!*" she yelled.

William's jaw dropped. "What the—?"

"*En garde!*" she yelled again and she lunged toward him, poking his own exposed erection with her plastic penis. Then she started swinging it side to side, slapping it against his erection as if they were swords parrying, causing the weirdest sword fight William had ever seen.

Swish swish swish!

William panicked and stumbled backwards. "Stop!"

Swish swish swish!

"Stop!"

She stood before the cowering William and stroked her fake penis victoriously with her fingertips. "Do you yield?"

"Stop that! Are you crazy?!"

She smiled. "No, I'm just having fun with this thing," she said and she wiggled her hips, causing the plastic penis to swing in a circular motion. "These things are great! You guys are so lucky!" She was beaming as she moved in and poked him again. "*Touché!*" Then she backed off.

William tried to protect himself with his hands. "Well, we don't do *that* with them!"

Mandi giggled. "You should. You could form leagues. Women would watch that."

William stared at her as if she was insane. He had no idea what to make of her, or if she was even serious. "I'm either in love with this girl or I hate her guts," he told himself.

"Can we get on with this please?" declared the woman.

Mandi and William both turned to face her. "Get on with what exactly?" asked William.

"Our photo shoot."

William pointed at Mandi's penis. "With that thing?"

"If you want the suit."

William glanced at the black suit and hung his

head.

—o—

William found himself on the bed on his knees. His skirt had been pulled up, exposing both his rear and his hard shaft. He wore no panties, so those weren't a problem. On his feet were still the same high heels he had worn all day. They trailed out behind him. Mandi was on her knees behind him, between his legs. She still wore the black mask. She was leaning over his back. He could feel the plastic penis touch his rear whenever she leaned forward. The photographer stood at the foot of the bed making adjustments to the camera. The woman was watching from a nearby chair. She had crossed her legs and was shaking one foot excitedly. Her nipples stood up beneath her dress.

"This is really exciting," said Mandi happily.

"Speak for yourself," said William sourly.

"Oh, don't tell me you aren't turned on."

"Hardly."

Mandi raised a doubtful eyebrow. Then she slipped her hand between his legs and grabbed his shaft from behind. It was hard as a rock. "*Hardly* is right," she laughed. "You're super turned on right now. I can even feel it throb. I could probably make you come with just a couple strokes. Wanna find out?"

"Absolutely not!"

Despite his objection, she gave him one quick stroke which made him tingle all over. Her hand was so soft and so warm and he was so excited that his manhood responded by throbbing right away.

"Stop that!" he exclaimed.

"Stop what?" she asked and she gave him another stroke. Her hand was sending intense pleasure waves to William's brain which were blasting through his body, zapping his strength and will to resist.

"Stop that!" he said again, though less forcefully.

Mandi heard the change and giggled. "Are you sure?"

She stroked him again. She could literally feel the pressure in his shaft.

"Yes, stop."

"Why?"

He was breathing hard now. "Because I don't want this."

"Yes, you do," she said and she stroked him twice this time.

"I don't." His objection was getting weaker.

Mandi snickered. "You are so turned on right now I'm surprised you haven't burst already."

William shook his head, but he was struggling. His eyes were closing. His body was screaming to let her finish. It felt so, so good. William was so turned on he could barely stand it, but he didn't want Mandi having this over him. She was already too much to handle, and she would get so much worse if she could claim to have made him come, especially the way they were posed. "N— no."

"Y— yeeees," she countered and she stroked him again.

He struggled to breathe. "S— stop," he whispered.

Mandi smiled. She was just about to finish him when another thought occurred. She slowed her hand to make sure he didn't come yet. "You know you like it... being all girly. That turns you on, doesn't it?"

"It doesn't."

"Yes, it does. We all know it."

He shook his head, which took incredible energy. "That's not true."

"Then why are you so hard? Why have you been

so hard all day?"

"Because I'm a guy and guys get hard."

Mandi laughed. "All right. If that's how you want it," she said and she pulled her hand away.

"Don't st—" he exclaimed before he caught himself.

A tense silence followed.

"Don't *stop*?" giggled Mandi finally. "Is that what you meant?"

William shook his head.

"'cause I'll start again if you tell me you're a cross-dresser."

William filled with conflict. Her hand had felt so good. Her strokes had felt amazing. It would have felt so good to let her finish him off. But on the hand... well, there was no other hand. Could he say that though? He dug deep and decided to—

"All right, let's get started again," said the woman as she finished marking the latest roll of film.

"Oh good!" said Mandi. She flicked the plastic penis with her finger, causing it to swing back and forth once more. "I've been waiting to use this!"

"Here's your chance," said the woman.

"What do we do?"

"Exactly what it looks like," said the woman.

"Which is what?" asked William.

"*This*," giggled Mandi and she leaned forward against his rear.

"Ahhhhhhh!" exclaimed William as the plastic device shoved its way past his cheeks inside him with no warning. William instantly recalled Professor Ivanova doing this to him. He recalled the embarrassment he felt, the pressure he felt, and the pleasure he felt when it hit the sweet spot. This time, it was Mandi doing it, and she rammed the device in faster and much more recklessly, upping all the stakes.

"You like that, don't you?" said Mandi.

"Not so fast!" he gasped. "Not so fast!"

Mandi laughed. "All right, I'll go slower." She pushed her body away from his, pulling the device almost all the way out.

"Ahhhhhh," said William again, this time sounding more relieved.

Mandi then pushed forwards once more.

"Ahhhhhh!"

Mandi giggled. "You squeal like a little girl."

"I do not!" protested William, but before he could complete that thought, Mandi pulled the device back out and rammed it back inside several times in quick succession, making him squeal like a girl once more.

"Ahhhhhh! uh ahhhhhhh!"

Mandi giggled.

And the photographer recorded it all.

—o—

An hour later, the shoot was over. William and Mandi were on their way home. They were being driven home by the woman's driver. William's new suit was in the trunk. He still wore the red kimono robe and the silver spike high heels he had worn for the pool portion of the shoot. He shifted uncomfortably on the seat. His rear was very sore. Mandi had worked him over mercilessly. He was embarrassed too. Mandi had worked him over mercilessly that way too. She sat on the seat next to him chuckling. She had had a great time. She held a stack of money in her hands.

"I can't believe we got paid for that!" giggled Mandi. She fanned herself with the bills. "I would do that again for free!"

"I'm glad you're happy," said William snidely.

He pulled back the kimono and peeked beneath it at the white bikini below. It seemed he had gotten a tan when they filmed the shots of him lounging by the pool in the bikini. "What kind of woman wears spike heels and a bikini?"

"You did."

"I know and I felt dirty doing it."

Mandi shrugged her shoulders. "You looked hot."

"Fortunately, no one will ever see that."

"Why are you so glum?" asked Mandi. "You got what you wanted. A suit. A little bit of money. You even came twice." This made William blush; he really wishes that hadn't happened, and yet it did, twice. "I honestly don't think you would have gotten a suit any other way, not at this late hour and without any money. Now you can go to your interview."

"If I can manage to sit down," countered William with some bitterness.

Mandi giggled. "Yeah, sorry. I guess I got carried away."

"'Carried away' is an understatement," said William and he rubbed his sore bottom. "You were like a piston in car engine."

Mandi blushed. "Yeah," she said wistfully. "Who knew those things were such fun?!"

"What things?"

Mandi held her hand out six or seven inches from her crotch. "*Those* things. Dicks. No wonder you boys are so obsessed with sex. It was like sword fighting, only no one could get hurt."

"My rear begs to differ."

"Don't give me that. You liked it, you squealed like a little girl! That was so funny. I wish I had that on tape. I'd make it your ring tone," said Mandi with a laugh, which made William shudder. "Well, let me tell you, any time you want to do that again, give me a call. I'm more than happy to ride you all over again."

"No, thank you!" said William dismissively and he waved his hand between them. "I'm done being a woman."

Mandi snickered. "We'll see."

William furrowed his brow. "What is that supposed to mean?"

"It means I think you like it too much to stop."

"I do not!"

"I think you do. You look great. You've got all the motions down. You make a great girl. You've done it for how many women now too? That just doesn't happen in real life. I think you like it. And I think you enjoyed everything that happened today, even if you won't admit it."

William blushed.

"So the next time you want to get your girl on, give me a ring. I know some clubs we can go to."

William sighed. Why were all the women in his life like this? Wasn't there some woman out there who didn't want to see him in a dress? Well, it didn't matter. He was done with women's clothes for the rest of his life. *Never again.* That was a promise. It was time to focus on the interview. Tomorrow was the big day. Tomorrow would change his life. He had his suit. He had his ride to the interview. He had his recommendation. He was ready.

Nothing could possibly go wrong...

The End... for now.

Thanks for reading my book!

Don't forget to check out my other books at my Amazon homepage:

https://www.amazon.com/Ann-Michelle/e/B007JLQ9RG/

—o—

Anything For An 'A'

William has a plan to keep from failing his college course. He's going to offer to do anything the gorgeous professor wants... anything. What could possibly go wrong there? Well, William is about to find out as he spends one very bad night in dresses.

—o—

Becoming Georgia (Part One: The New Maid)

George and his friend Oliver thought no one was watching when they accidentally broke the window playing ball. Little did they know that George's pesky stepsister Emma saw the whole thing. Now they would find out what the price was for her silence. Much to their surprise... it involves dresses.

—o—

Becoming Georgia (Part Two: The Mall)

Poor George. After getting caught breaking Widow Wilson's window, he finds himself firmly under Emma's thumb as she blackmails him to get whatever she wants. And what does she want? She wants him to do her chores. She likes to see him jump at her command. And perhaps worst of all, she likes to dress him in her clothes. Now he's been caught in a compromising position by Emma and her guests. Things could not get worse, could they? Sadly, they can. This is the story of George's trip to the mall.

—o—

Becoming Georgia (Part Three: Servitude)

George's story continues. With his stepmother discovering the clothes Emma bought him, George now finds himself sentenced to remain a girl full-time for the foreseeable future. What's more, when his stepmother learns he broke Widow Wilson's window, she orders him to work off the cost of the window as Wilson's maid. At least he's free of Emma's domination, right? Well, maybe not.

In this third part of George's story, George struggles with being dressed as a girl full-time while trying to understand why this is all becoming more and more normal for him. This is Part Three of the series.

—o—

Blackmailed Sissy Maid

Powerful men like Christopher Jordan need ways to unwind. For Christopher this meant having a safe, anonymous internet mistress. But this mistress wasn't as anonymous as he thought. Christopher will now learn a hard lesson as this mysterious mistress slowly places him at the mercy of the women in his life.

—o—

Caught By His Roommate

Mitch thought Katie was the perfect woman. She was beautiful. She was innocent. She was naive. And best of all, she dressed the way young women should dress in heels and dresses. So Mitch tricked Katie into becoming roommates so he could explore her closet. Unfortunately for

Mitch, Katie would catch him red handed. That's when things got really strange for Mitch. See, Katie wasn't as innocent and naive as he thought, and she had plans for her new sissy!

This book includes Five Illustrations!!

— o —

Caught By His Wife's Best Friend (Part One)

While Dylan's wife was away on a business trip, Dylan decided to spend a little time playing in her closet. Unfortunately for him, his wife's friend Colby catches him. Naturally, she wants to have some fun with Dylan, which means blackmail and feminization. How far will Colby go? Will Dylan's wife figure it out?

— o —

Caught By His Wife's Best Friend (Part Two)

Dylan wasn't all that upset to find himself blackmailed by his wife's best friend Colby after she caught him cross-dressing. After all, this was the fantasy of a lifetime come true. But with Colby's demands becoming ever greater, Dylan finally had no choice but to try to escape her power. So he called his wife. Yep. *He called his wife!* What will happen now? Will she save her husband from Colby? And will there be a price to pay for her help? Maybe Dylan will end up a feminized secretary after all.

— o —

Caught In Her Closet

Jimmy always enjoyed cross-dressing secretly when no one else was home. Then he gets caught by Christine and her friend. What will Christine do with her new stepsissy?

With five illustrations from Ilgor!

—o—

A Collection of Short Stories, Vol. One: Three Tales of Halloween Magic

Sometimes, stories are better when they are short and sweet. This first volume of short stories includes three separate tales of Halloween magic:

They Messed With The Wrong Witch: Three rotten brothers learn a lesson they will never forget when they wrongly accuse a woman of being a witch.

The Magic Ring: A husband and wife argue over a magic ring only to discover that magic can be a dangerous and tricky thing. Soon they learn what happens when the shoe ends up on the other foot.

I Wasn't Myself: The tale of a man who finds himself in the body of his ex-wife. That's not the worst part though. The worst part is that his ex-wife is now in his!

—o—

A Collection of Short Stories, Vol. Two: Tales of Feminization By Hypnosis

Sometimes, stories are better when they are short and sweet. This second volume of short stories includes four tales of feminization by hypnosis!

Save Us Sis!: Candice gets a plea from her brother to come save him and their father. Is this a joke? Or is something sinister going on at home?

Controlled By His Roommate: Dave is about to learn that his roommate Katie has more control over him than he thought!

The 'Disappearance' of Alpha Mu: A college committee investigates the 'disappearance' of Alpha Mu fraternity. Though, 'disappearance' might be the wrong word.

Hypnotized Husband: Diane is shocked when her husband starts dressing like a woman after he participates in a hypnosis stage show. But all may not be as it seems.

— o —

Dress Coded

Written in the spirit of *Grounded in Heels*, this is the story of Charlie Mitchell. Charlie wants to wear shorts, but the dress code doesn't allow it. He tries it anyway, figuring that the worst the principal can do is send him home for the day. Boy, was he wrong! Before he knows it, Charlie finds himself stuck in skirts and dresses and worse. What will the other students think? Will this complicate his run for class president against his nemesis... Stephanie Mills?

— o —

Emasculated By His Mother-in-Law (Part One)

Richard agreed to help his pregnant wife Christine fit a dress. In the middle of doing so, however, his wife's mother unexpectedly shows up and catches him in the dress! The only way for Richard and Christine to avoid utter embarrassment, and years of nagging from Christine's mother, is if Richard pretends he's really the maid until she leaves. Unfortunately, his mother-in-law has no plans to leave. What's more, she sees through the charade and decides this might be a good opportunity to teach Richard some lessons. Things may not turn out as anyone expects though.

—o—

Emasculated By His Mother-in-Law (Part Two)

Martha's attempt to teach Richard and Christine a lesson has backfired. Trapping Richard as Miranda has given him the chance to see that maybe there is something exciting about being feminized after all. But will Richard take Miranda as far as Christine wants? And how far will Martha go to put an end to this charade?

—o—

Emasculated By His Mother-in-Law (Part Three)

Trapped cross-dressed by his mother-in-law's unexpected appearance, Richard and his wife Christine undertook an ill-considered deception to keep from having to explain why he was dressed the way he was. It seemed simple enough. But now Richard finds himself stuck living as his wife's maid and every day seems to dig him deeper into the charade. And as if that wasn't enough, now his sister-in-law has shown up as well and she knows his secret! These are hard times for Richard... at least until the hormones kick in. But then, maybe he's enjoying it? See how things turn out for Richard and Christine in this lengthy conclusion!

—o—

Emasculating My Husband

When I married Mike, I thought I had found my fairy-tale prince. He seemed to be strong and confident and the kind of man you wanted to lead the family you hoped to build. Sadly, I soon learned that he was none of those things. Still, I did my best to be the submissive little housewife I had been taught to be. Then one day, just as I could take no more, I came upon a hormone cream that would change everything. Before my plans were finished, Mike would be the submissive little housewife in the four-inch heels!

— o —
Femford School for Girls (Part One)

Lewis Stevens thinks his fiancée is having an affair at the secretive girl's school where she works. He decides to sneak into the school to find out. Little does he realize that this girl's school has another purpose. Now he finds himself trapped and going through their program. Can his fiancée help him? Will she want to?

— o —
The Femford School (Part Two)

Each day Lewis remains trapped at the Femford School, he finds himself feminized further. Bit by bit, his masculinity is being stripped away. What's more, Vera has set into motion a series of changes that will forever alter Lewis's mind and body to make him Maria's submissive pet. Only Maria can save him now, but why does she keep dragging her feet? Can Lewis resist long enough to convince her to save his manhood?

— o —
Feminized and Cuckolded

Brent watches as his new boss Rebecca seduces and marries his friend John. Before Brent's very eyes, she begins to feminize his friend. So why doesn't Brent do something to stop her? Well, it's complicated. See, he wants her for himself, and if John becomes a girl, that might make it easier. This can't end well.

— o —
Feminized By His Mother-in-Law: Part One: Not Man Enough

Christopher has a problem. He has a beautiful new wife

who loves him, but his mother-in-law thinks he's not man enough for her. Even worse, she's set out to prove it. Can Christopher stop her from making him not a man at all?

—o—

Feminized By His Mother-in-Law: Part Two: Not Woman Enough

Christopher's problem is getting worse. Not only is his mother-in-law still determined to prove that he's not man enough for his wife, but now his wife is starting to think she wants him feminized. Can 'Chrissy' escape his increasingly feminine fate?

—o—

Feminized By Hypnosis

Jess and his stepmother never got along, at least until she brought him a new CD. Now they get along great. What's more, Jess and his father have decided to clean up their acts... to be more helpful. They're even wearing maid uniforms to help around the house. So why does something about this seem wrong to Jess? Can Jess find help to save him from his evil stepmother, or are he and his father destined to become sissy maids... or worse?

—o—

Feminized Cuckold

When powerbroker Paul Jackson loses his job, he finds himself at the mercy of his trophy wife. Little by little, she feminizes Paul as she turns him from domineering husband into submissive housewife. She even invites his former best friend to move into their home, and she cuckolds him. Will this be his new life or can he escape his fate?

—o—

Feminized Fiancé

When Victoria Martin built 'The Martin Firm' into one of the most prestigious firms in the world, she expected that her daughter Sarah would one day follow in her high-heeled footsteps and take over the business. When she learns that Sarah is planning to marry a young man Victoria considers entirely unsuitable, however, Victoria sets out to make sure Sarah will never want to marry him... by turning him into a woman.

—o—

Serving His Fiancée

Rick is now trapped in a rigged bet with the powerful Victoria Martin. Rick must win his fiancée back to regain his freedom or he'll be trapped as Victoria's sissy maid forever! Complicating Rick's plight, Victoria is forcing him to masquerade as his fiancée's personal maid 'Sissy', and he can't tell her who he really is. But does she already know?

—o—

Feminizing Her Husband (The Complete Story – Parts 1 & 2)

Part One: How Megan Avoided Pregnancy: Megan and Mark can't agree. Mark wants a baby, but Megan does not. When Mark issues an ultimatum to his wife demanding a baby, she counters by demanding that he dress as a woman for nine months before she will agree to get pregnant. Naturally, she assumes her macho husband will never agree. Imagine her surprise when he does. What follows is a cat and mouse game as each tries to trick the other into giving up.

Part Two: How Megan Got Pregnant: Things are changing fast now as Mark begins to 'grow' into the role of 'Princess.'

But Mark isn't the only one changing. Megan is about to undergo a major change as well. Will Mark get the baby he wants? Will Megan let him escape with his masculinity intact?

— o —

Grounded in Heels

When Sam's stepmother discovers the perfect way to keep her stepson out of trouble, she unknowingly puts him at the mercy of his worst enemy... his vengeful stepsister Diane. Now Diane has plans to make sure he never escapes. Can Sam find a way to save himself or will his summer in heels become a lifetime sentence?

— o —

Grounded In Heels (Part Two: Back To School)

With Sam's stepmother forcing Sam to return to school as 'Samantha' until she can find a way to undo the feminine changes Diane has done to his body, Sam must learn to deal with being a young woman surrounded by the people who knew him as Sam. Can he keep his secret? Even worse, Sam still finds himself under the absolutely power of his vengeful stepsister Diane, who is determined to humiliate him and make his time in heels permanent.

— o —

Her High-Heeled Solution

John's wife Suzie wrongly thinks she's caught her husband having an affair. With the help of a friend, she comes up with an ingenious way to guarantee that John will never have another affair: she locks him into a pair of high heels. This simple solution goes wrong, however, as husband and wife both try to outwit each other. Soon events are spinning out of control. What's more, standing in the middle of all of this is Crystal, Suzie's best friend, who is having a grand time manipulating them both to make sure John gets slowly feminized.

— o —

The House On Femford Hill

Would you stay in a haunted house? What if the house was known for turning men into women? Professor Eric Meyer plans to stay. See, Professor Meyer studies the strange, the supernatural, and the paranormal, and he can't wait to investigate the famed House on Femford Hill, which is rumored to turn those who stay overnight into women. Could this be true? Professor Meyer intends to find out.

Includes a surprise re-edited story from Crystal Summers!

— o —

Humiliation At The Office

For too long, corporate hotshot Andrew Boden treated the women of the office like sex objects. Now his secretary is out to settle the score as she slowly feminizes him and traps him in an inescapable web of femininity and humiliation. Little by little, Andrew loses his power, his freedom, and his masculinity, and everyone at the office is noticing.

— o —

The Making of Danielle (Parts One Through Five)

This is my take on a very classic idea that comes up often in our genre: the idea of the young man transformed by an evil "Aunt." It's also my biggest selling series!

Daniel is an unruly young man who fights constantly with his stepmother. To end the fighting once and for all, his stepmother sends Daniel to an Aunt he's never met who will teach him discipline. Imagine his surprise when he finds himself put into skirts and he is trained to become a girl.

—o—

The Story of William, From The Making of Danielle

I've been promising to add something special to the "Making of Danielle" series, and here it is! This is the story of William and how he was transformed into Wilma. These are the things Daniel never knew. *It is also the conclusion to Daniel's story.* How does Daniel's story end? In a word: a wedding. To whom is the question though! Fans of Danielle really won't want to miss this one.

—o—

Miss-ing Billionaire

Reporter Martin Ward has uncovered an incredible story. The billionaire founder of Ing Co. is missing, and Martin's source tells him the billionaire's new wife is behind it. Unfortunately, the only way Martin can investigate this story is to disguise himself as a woman and to infiltrate the strange world of Ing Co. But do they know who he is?

—o—

More Than He Bargained For

Jeff wanted to change his wife. He wanted her to be more adventurous in the bedroom, so he took a long shot on some hypnosis tapes. Only, she found out what he was doing. That's when she decided to teach him a lesson he would never forget by giving him exactly what he wants and so much more. His life at home and at the office will never be the same. (This includes the alternate cuckold ending as a bonus.)

—o—

My Femdom Marriage (Part One)

This is the true story of how my wife took over our marriage and made me her feminized slave.

−o−

My Femdom Marriage (Part Two)

This is the rest of the true story of how my wife took over our marriage and feminized me.

−o−

My Lactating Husband (Part One)

What would you do if you started growing breasts? That's the problem Andrew faces. His life was great. He had a loving wife and a good job. He was even up for a promotion. Then he took an experimental treatment meant to grow hair... but something else grew instead. As his chest slowly expands into a pair of classic breasts, he finds his wife taking over and himself demoted. What's more, his boss wants him to report to work as a secretary! Where will this end?

−o−

My Lactating Husband (Part Two)

Things are really headed in the wrong direction now for Andrew. Not only can he no longer hide the "growths" on his chest, but now he needs to report to work as a secretary... dressed as a woman. Even worse, his new boss is not exactly the nicest woman. How bad can she be though? Andrew is about to find out. Hopefully, he can remember the things his wife taught him about being a woman.

−o−

Satin Falls (The Complete Story, Parts One & Two

Combined)

Satin Falls is the story of a small mountain town where the men slowly lose their ability to resist any command given by any woman after an unknown virus infects the water supply. Even worse, advising the women on how to handle this is a psychiatrist with a grudge against men after her female lover leaves her for a man. She decides to get even with *male*kind by encouraging the women to feminize their males.

Follow the lives of several couples as they enter this brave new world of silks and satins and female domination. And watch as the fate of the men hangs by the well-manicured fingertips of one young woman.

—o—

Short Story: The Magic Journal

After macho football player Brad ruins Rachel's date, she gets even using a magic journal which lets her change his body as she wishes. Brad is about to learn a lesson he will never forget as Rachel feminizes him bit by bit.

—o—

Summer in Skirts (Part One: Becoming Summer)

Paul is sent to spend the summer with a crazy old acquaintance of his parents. He's not too happy about it either. Making matters worse, he finds a pair of twins already living there, and they have designs on him. They seem to think he should be obeying them. Naturally, he has a different view on the matter. Before long, they teach him the meaning of petticoat punishment. Things go increasingly more wrong – or right – from there.

—o—

Summer in Skirts (Part Two: Queen of the Fair)

Now that Paul is firmly stuck as 'Summer' for the rest of the summer, it's time he explored his new relationship with the wonderful Ellie. Unfortunately, the twins are about to take center stage in his life again, and Paul isn't going to escape them this time. Ellie has a plan, however, but Paul isn't going to like it.

—o—

Two Weeks As His Wife's Feminized Submissive

Paul has a secret. While Paul appears to be a man in charge, his wife Amanda is the one who really holds the power... ever since she caught him cross-dressing. Now she wears the pants in the family. What's more, for two weeks every year, Amanda turns Paul into Paula, her feminized, submissive plaything.

—o—

Wager Into Womanhood (The Complete Story – Parts 1 & 2)

Max is an arrogant sexist with a submissive wife and an inability to turn down any bet. Will is a househusband with a dominant wife who just caught him having an affair. Both of their lives are going to change significantly when they get tricked into entering a bet to prove that they can live as women for a week... or longer.

—o—

The Writer's Secret

Loren had no idea what he was getting into when his agent suggested he write transvestite fiction. If that's what sold, then he would give it a try. Then he told his wife Stephanie. Soon, he and his loving wife were experimenting with turning him into 'Lauren.' Too late did he realize how eagerly his wife would embrace the idea of feminizing him.

— o —

The Writer's Secret (Part Two: Blackmailed Sissy)

Loren and Stephanie's adventure continues in this long awaited sequel to "The Writer's Secret"!

As Loren adjusts to living as a woman, his life becomes complicated when a young relative of Stephanie's comes to stay with them. This seemingly sweet and naive young woman turns out to have an unexpected dark side and a penchant for blackmail... and she likes the idea of having a feminized maid. At the same time, Stephanie faces a boss who demands that she sleep with him if she wants to keep her job. How will Loren and Stephanie escape these villains?

— o —

Volume One of the Dominique Silk Collection

This first Volume One of Dominique Silk stories includes both *College Student to Coed* and *Making Her Husband Her Maid*.

College Student to Coed is the story of poor Ted, who can't believe his luck when the most popular girl on campus, Beth Armstrong, hits on him. Even better, she wants to take him back to her apartment and dress him in her clothes! This is a dream come true for Ted, and soon Beth is inviting him over daily to play. Unfortunately, through a series of mistakes, Ted finds himself constantly being exposed in public while wearing women's clothes. But are these really mistakes? And what is Beth up to?

Making Her Husband Her Maid is a cautionary tale for

unfaithful husbands. As Diane works hard to support the family, her husband Cameron seduces the maid. Unfortunately for him, the maid has other ideas and turns the tables on Cameron. Imagine Diane's surprise to come home to find her husband dressed in the maid's uniform and high heels, and bent over the couch as the maid has her way with his rear. Cameron the playboy is about to become Camilla the maid.

— o —

Volume Two of the Dominique Silk Collection

This Volume Two of Dominique Silk stories is both parts of *Feminized by his Mother-in-Law*, the story of Jackson, his wife Natalie, and his mother-in-law Ruth. Ruth never thought that Jackson was man enough to marry her daughter, and when she came to stay with Jackson and Natalie shortly after their marriage, she decided to prove this to her daughter... by feminizing Jackson. Has she miscalculated though? Soon *both* Ruth and Natalie are feminizing Jackson. He even finds himself sent on a date with Natalie's boss and ends up helping him seduce her! Can Jackson save his manhood and his marriage?

— o —

Volume Three of the Dominique Silk Collection

This Volume Three of Dominique Silk stories includes both *The Sissy House Sitter* and *Cuckolded Sissified Quarterback*.

The Sissy House Sitter begins when Louis is offered a chance to house sit for his stunningly sexy neighbor Brandy and her husband. He jumps at it for one reason: he wants to explore her closet. This is a dream come true for Louis who feels an irresistible pull from feminine clothing. Things get really interesting for Louis, however, when he finds certain home movies made by Brandy and her husband... but not as interesting as when Brandy comes home early and catches Louis in her husband's dress.

Cuckolded Sissified Quarterback is the story of Brady Hunter. He's the star quarterback for a top professional team, but his body is slowly wearing out. He decides to take steroids so he can play just one more year. Unfortunately for Brady, his gold-digging wife catches him and she decides to take advantage of her discovery by blackmailing him. She feminizes him, humiliates him, and then cuckolds him with a younger player with better prospects. Will Brady manage to get back out onto the field or is his future to be submissive in skirts?

— o —

Volume Four of the Dominique Silk Collection

This final Volume Four of Dominique Silk stories includes the story **Not What He Wanted** and its conclusion **What He Got**. This story begins with George trying to dominate his wife. Things go wrong quickly, however, and he finds himself on the wrong side of the velvet ropes. Soon, he's wearing panties at work... and then worse. As his wife keeps adding to his feminization, an embarrassing trip to the mall and a confrontation with his secretary await. Hopefully, you'll find poor George's story fun and exciting as his problems spin out of control.